Brody continued to grip her hand as if he feared she'd ignore his request.

Drawn to the controlled strength of his hold, she glanced up once again, finding his gaze haunting. There was something under the surface that Brody wasn't willing to share, something more than his concern for an injured soldier. In that fleeting moment, she glimpsed an unspoken need. For what, she wasn't sure.

A flash of awareness passed between them. He pulled in a breath and released her hand.

The separation jarred her. Surely she hadn't wanted him to continue holding her hand. Or had she?

Surprised and angered when tears pooled in her eyes, she blinked them back. What was it about this man that caused such a mix of emotion to well up within her?

Books by Debby Giusti

DEBBY GIUSTI

is a medical technologist who loves working with test tubes and petri dishes almost as much as she loves to write. Growing up as an army brat, Debby met and married her husband—then a captain in the army—at Fort Knox, Kentucky. Together they traveled the world, raised three wonderful army brats of their own and have now settled in Atlanta, Georgia, where Debby spins tales of suspense that touch the heart and soul. Contact Debby through her website, www.debbygiusti.com, email debby@debbygiusti.com, or write c/o Love Inspired Suspense, 233 Broadway, Suite 1001, New York, NY 10279.

THE SOLDIER'S SISTER

DEBBY GIUSTI

HARLEQUIN® LOVE INSPIRED® SUSPENSE

Recycling programs for this product may not exist in your area.

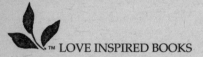 ™ LOVE INSPIRED BOOKS

ISBN-13: 978-0-373-67574-6

THE SOLDIER'S SISTER

www.LoveInspiredBooks.com

Printed in U.S.A.

Glorify the Lord with me;
let us exalt his name together.

I sought the Lord, and he answered me;
he delivered me from all my fears.
—*Psalms* 34:3–4

Heartfelt thanks to

Ann Yingling,
AW2 Advocate,
Atlanta Metropolitan Area and North Georgia,
and
Nancy Carlisle,
AW2 Advocate,
Fort Benning, Georgia,
for providing invaluable information about the
Army Wounded Warrior Program.

With gratitude to
LTC Stony Lohr, U.S. Army Retired,
for his help with the
Military Investigations series.

ONE

The gathering dark clouds had mirrored Stephanie Upton's mood since she'd returned home to Freemont, Georgia, two days earlier. Grateful as she was to get the job as the Army Wounded Warrior advocate at nearby Fort Rickman where her brother Ted was convalescing from his war injuries, she was frustrated that he had refused to see her or answer her phone calls.

So much for a happy homecoming.

The August storm hit just as she left town, heading back to post. She leaned forward in the driver's seat, wishing she'd replaced the old windshield wipers that failed to clear the heavy downpour. Squinting, she could barely make out the yellow dividing line on the road.

A small strip mall appeared in the distance. She turned her Corolla into the parking lot to wait out the deluge and reached for her cell phone. Glancing at her client file on the passenger seat, she tapped in the number for Private First Class Joshua Webb and smiled, remembering her younger brother's high school friend.

"Joshua, this is Stephanie Upton, Ted's sister," she

said when the call went to voice mail. "I'm back in town and took the position at Fort Rickman as the AW2—Army Wounded Warrior—advocate. I know this is short notice, but you're on my caseload. Since we need to schedule an appointment, I thought I'd stop by now while I'm the neighborhood and see how you're doing."

She glanced at her watch. "I'm about ten minutes from your house. As soon as the rain lets up, I'll head your way. Looking forward to seeing you soon."

Joshua and Ted had served in the same unit in Afghanistan and both had been injured by an IED. Josh had lost his legs, while her brother had sustained burns on his stomach and lower extremities. The two friends had been medically evacuated to hospitals in the United States and finally sent back to Fort Rickman.

Eventually, Josh would learn to walk with prosthetic legs, but for now he was wheelchair bound, which was probably the reason he hadn't answered her call. Hopefully, he would retrieve the message before she arrived on his doorstep.

Three years ago and just a few weeks after both guys had graduated from high school, Stephanie had left Freemont, never expecting to return. At least not so soon. Over time her feelings had mellowed and eventually taken a backseat to helping her brother through his current recuperation.

Ted had been headstrong and difficult to handle in his teen years. She had hoped his stint in the military would be a positive influence. Although she didn't need an abundance of brotherly love, she had expected civility and a glimmer of hope that with time they could eventually heal the past.

The one bright note was the warm and enthusiastic welcome from the folks with whom she would be working at Fort Rickman. Stephanie had held a similar position as the advocate for wounded soldiers at Fort Stewart, a three-hour drive east, and was well aware of the importance of making initial contact with the military personnel on her caseload.

She had visited two soldiers in Freemont this morning and had planned to stop by Josh's house on her way back to Fort Rickman. Seeing Ted's old friend would be an opportunity to catch up on Josh's plans for the future. As a teen, he had always been optimistic and upbeat. In spite of his recent injury, she hoped he retained the zest for life that had endeared him to her as a kid.

As soon as the rain eased, she pulled back onto Freemont Road and headed south. Ten minutes later, she saw the sign for Josh's subdivision.

She put on her signal, and just before she made the turn, a pickup truck perched on oversize tires screeched around the corner, its rear end fishtailing on the slick pavement.

The truck flew past—narrowly missing her car— in a blur of red paint and steel chrome. Muddy water, kicked up from the big, knobby tires, shot through the air, streaking Georgia clay across her windshield.

She laid on the horn and glanced in the rearview

mirror as the truck crested a rise in the road and then disappeared from sight.

Her heart pounded like a reverberating snare drum, its cadence keeping time with the tension that throbbed across her forehead as she realized how close she'd come to a collision. Pulling in a number of cleansing breaths, she turned into the Cypress Springs subdivision, determined to focus on her visit with Joshua instead of the runaway truck.

Although the rain had stopped, the sky remained dismal and gray. She swerved around a scattering of leaves and twigs that littered the roadway and parked in front of the last house on the end of one of the side streets, a modest ranch Joshua was renovating to be wheelchair accessible.

Curb appeal and a low price tag made the neighborhood of new homes a great buy for a returning soldier starting over. As Josh's advocate, she should have felt a surge of elation that he was focusing on his transition to civilian life, but all Stephanie could think about was her own close call and her rapid pulse that failed to calm.

Grabbing her purse, she stepped onto the sidewalk, closing the car door behind her. A gust of humid air tugged at her skirt as she headed toward the house, her heels clipping along the sidewalk. She pulled her damp hair back from her face and climbed the ramp to the tiny front stoop.

The enthusiastic voice of a sports announcer sounded from inside the house. The full-blast volume of the radio drowned out her knocks on the door.

When Joshua failed to answer, she tried the knob. Locked. Surely he hadn't left the house with the radio blaring.

"Josh?"

Determined to be heard, she pounded on the door again and again, to no avail. Finally, letting out a frustrated breath, she headed around the corner to the kitchen entrance, where a second sheet of plywood served as a wheelchair ramp.

The sound of the ball game spewed through the back door that hung open, sending another round of concern tangling along her spine. Flicking her gaze over the backyard, she searched for some sign of the injured soldier.

"It's Stephanie Upton," she called, aware of the nervous tremble in her voice as she stepped inside. "Can you hear me, Josh?"

The smell of fresh paint and new carpet greeted her, along with the announcer's voice echoing through the empty rooms.

She paused in the middle of the kitchen, straining to hear something, anything other than the backdrop of cheering baseball fans.

Running water?

She raised her brow. "Joshua?"

A flutter of new fear flowed over her. The hair on her arms prickled as she peered into the living-dining combination straight ahead.

"Braves six, Astros two."

"Josh?"

Turning left, she entered the hallway that led to the rear of the house.

"It's the top of the fifth with Atlanta in the lead."

Her neck tingled. A double amputee bound to a wheelchair brought to mind all sorts of scenarios.

Hopefully, he wasn't hurt.

The announcer's voice sounded over the rush of water. Glancing into the bathroom on the right, she gasped. Her hand flew to her throat.

Joshua lay on the floor fully clothed, his body crumpled next to an overturned wheelchair and surrounded by sharp shards of a broken vanity mirror. Blood pooled under his left arm. The cloying smell filled the tiny room.

Water gushed from the spigot into the rapidly filling tub. Aware that someone else could be in the house, yet terrified for Joshua's well-being, she turned off the faucet and dropped to her knees beside the soldier. His face was pale as death, his eyes glassed over. She searched for the artery in his neck and groaned with relief when she found a faint but steady pulse.

"Josh, can you hear me?" Stephanie raised the sleeve of his blood-soaked shirt and almost heaved. Rich, red blood pulsed from the deep gash on his upper arm.

Frantic, she dug in her purse for her cell phone and hit the programmed nine-one-one.

"State your emergency." The operator's monotone drawl was barely audible over the sports announcer's booming voice.

Balancing the phone between her shoulder and ear,

Stephanie groped her hand along the bathroom vanity, found the docked iPod and turned off the game.

"There's been an accident." Stretching, she grabbed a towel from the overhead rack and jammed the thick terry against the open wound. "A man's been cut by glass. He's bleeding and needs medical attention. Tell the EMTs to hurry."

"What's your address?"

"One-forty-something Cedar Springs Drive. Third house on the right."

"I need the house number, ma'am. Could you check outside?"

Josh's breathing was shallow. His partially opened eyes appeared dull and lifeless. She wanted to scream at the woman on the other end of the line who failed to recognize the severity of the situation.

"Operator, I'm trying to keep this man from bleeding to death. I can't leave him. Get an ambulance and get it here fast."

She clicked off and speed dialed Joshua's unit at Fort Rickman. A deep male voice answered on the second ring.

"WTB."

"Major Jenkins?"

"No, ma'am. This is Special Agent Brody Goodman with the Criminal Investigation Division on post."

Her eyes widened. "I dialed the CID?"

"You dialed one of the units on post, namely the Warrior Transitional Battalion. Major Jenkins is out of the office at the moment and asked me to catch the phone. May I take a message or have the major call you back?"

"Tell him Stephanie Upton phoned. I'm the new AW2 advocate." Her breath hitched. "One of the men on my caseload—Private First Class Joshua Webb—fell from his wheelchair and cut his arm. He's lost a significant amount of blood. An ambulance is on the way."

"Give me the address."

Once again, she relayed directions to the small house.

"Major Jenkins just stepped back into the office. I'll fill him in on the emergency. Hold tight, ma'am. We're heading your way and should be there shortly."

Stephanie didn't know Brody Goodman with the calm voice and take-charge attitude. Nor had she previously dealt with anyone in the CID. Usually they handled serious crimes on post. Perhaps Special Agent Goodman and Major Jenkins were friends or working together on a special project. She had only yesterday met the executive officer for the Warrior Transitional Battalion, but she felt a sense of relief that the two men would soon be en route.

"Josh." Her brother's voice sounded from the front of the house.

Glad for help, she called, "He's in the bathroom, Ted."

"Someone's there with you?" the CID agent asked.

"Another soldier. I can't talk, Agent Goodman. Get here as soon as you can." Unable to stem the flow of blood, she dropped the cell to the tile floor and, using both hands, pushed even harder on the towel.

Footsteps sounded in the hallway.

Ted appeared in the open doorway, his slender face pulled tight. Confusion, then anger, flashed from his eyes. "What did you do to him, Stephanie?"

Hurt by his accusation, she pursed her lips. "I didn't do anything. He fell. An ambulance should be here soon. Go outside and flag down the EMTs when they turn onto the street."

"I'm not leaving Josh." Her brother knelt beside her. "Let me hold the towel."

"I've got it."

"Just like you had Hayden? You let him die. I won't let you kill Josh, too."

"Ted, please." Why did he have to bring up their painful past in the middle of this crisis?

"Please what, Stephanie? Forget about what happened? I told you never to come back to Freemont."

Her stomach roiled. No matter what she did, her relationship with her brother would never change.

"Ms. Upton, answer me. Are you all right?"

Hearing the agent's urgent voice, she raised the cell to her ear again. "I'm sorry. I…I thought I had disconnected." She glanced down at the stained towel. "I'm okay."

But she really wasn't. She'd nearly had a fatal collision with a psycho driver just a short while earlier. Now Joshua's life was slipping away as she watched.

"Hurry," she finally warned. "Before things get any worse."

* * *

"What do you know about the new AW2 advocate?" Brody asked as he drove out the Fort Rickman main gate and headed north along Freemont Road. Recalling the urgency in Stephanie Upton's voice, he pushed down on the accelerator.

Major Jenkins sat next to him, equally worried about the situation. "She held the same position at Fort Stewart. Our former advocate had some unexpected medical problems and had to retire. Stephanie transferred here to fill the vacancy."

"And PFC Webb?"

"Lost both his legs in an IED explosion in Afghanistan."

Brody shook his head, feeling the frustration of too many young men and women being injured in the line of duty. Casualties were a horrific by-product of war. Not what he or anyone associated with the military wanted.

"Joshua Webb was initially treated at Walter Reed," the major said, "and was recently assigned to Fort Rickman."

"Do you have anyone named Ted in your battalion?" Jenkins nodded. "Ted Upton."

"Related to the advocate?"

"Ted's her brother. He was in the same convoy that hit the IED. Upton was burned and treated at the Army Burn Center at Fort Sam Houston."

"Now they're home, getting ready to transition out of the military?"

"Private Webb will probably get a medical discharge. He's waiting for his new prostheses. Upton has the option of returning to active duty. The burns have healed, but he's still in counseling."

Brody raised his brow. "Over the phone, he sounded antagonistic toward his sister."

"I don't know anything about their relationship. I met her yesterday so it's just a first impression, but she seemed levelheaded and competent. PFC Upton's like a lot of other soldiers. He's young and wondering what the future will hold."

"What about Webb?"

Jenkins smiled. "PFC Webb's got a strong faith and a desire to make a difference in life. He'll do okay."

Your faith will sustain you, folks had told Brody nine years ago. *Lean on the Lord,* a statement he never understood. Why would he lean on a God who had let him down so tragically?

Brody shoved the thought aside. "What's your take on Upton? Is he stable?"

"His squad leader and first sergeant say he's guarded and doesn't readily share his feelings. The counselors encourage the soldiers to talk about their problems."

"Just as you and I had discussed earlier in conjunction with post-traumatic stress disorder."

The major nodded. "Exactly."

"What does the doc say about Upton?"

"That he needs more counseling."

The entrance to the Cedar Springs area appeared on the left. Brody turned into the subdivision littered with debris from the storm and made a right at the third street. At the end of the road, two Freemont black-

and-whites sat curbside, their lights flashing. An ambulance had backed into the driveway. Its rear door hung open. A gray Chevy and an older-model Corolla were parked nearby.

Brody led the way into the house, glancing first at the police officer and then at the tall, slender woman standing near the fireplace. Arms wrapped defensively around her waist, she turned as he stepped forward, her eyes as blue as the sky and strangely haunting. The furrow of her brow and the downward tug on her full lips provided a glimpse of the concern she felt for the injured soldier.

Her pastel skirt was smeared with blood, her blouse, as well. A crusty streak lined her pale cheek. If the victim's injury hadn't been accidental, the blood-spattered advocate might be a likely suspect, but her reason for visiting the soldier seemed legit.

Confusion covered her face, probably due to the shock of finding the injured victim. Images of the scene he had walked into nine years ago replayed through his memory. His breath caught in his chest. Sweat broke out on his upper lip. He clamped down his jaw and forced the image to flee, just as he'd done a thousand times before. Today he needed to focus on the woman with the questioning eyes that bored into his soul.

She looked at him the way Lisa had. After all these years, he still needed to guard himself against the pain. More than anything, he never wanted to be vulnerable again. Especially to someone who reminded him of the woman he had loved and lost.

A young man leaned against the counter in the kitchen. The guy wore cargo pants and flip-flops with an army T-shirt. From the high, tight haircut and the splotch of angry, red skin on his left arm, he was more than likely the advocate's younger brother.

His right hand was bandaged. Blood spotted his shirt. The wail of accusation Brody had heard over the phone replayed in his mind.

Seeing his commanding officer, the kid pulled himself upright. "Afternoon, Major Jenkins." He raised his injured hand to his forehead. "Thanks for coming, sir."

"How are you doing, Ted?"

The kid nodded a bit too enthusiastically. "Fine, sir."

While Jenkins talked to Private Upton, Brody continued into the hallway, where a transport stretcher filled the narrow space. Moving past the obstruction, he looked into the bathroom. Two EMTs, one male, one female, knelt over the victim.

Brody flashed his badge at the cop standing at the side of the doorway. "CID, Fort Rickman."

The Freemont policeman nodded. "Didn't take you long to get here from post."

"What do you have?" Brody pressed, uninterested in small talk.

"Joshua Webb was renovating his house along with his friend, Ted Upton. The guy's in the kitchen. He's pretty shook-up."

"You questioned him?"

"Briefly. Seems they were trying to install a new vanity mirror that dropped and shattered. Ted Upton cut his hand. Joshua insisted he have it checked out at the hospital. When Ted returned, the woman was on the floor next to Joshua, using a towel to stop his bleeding. She called nine-one-one."

Josh Webb appeared to be physically fit other than his missing limbs. Short hair, youthful face, strong upper body. His wheelchair lay on its side.

"Looks like he was trying to clean up the broken glass, maybe extended his reach too far, and fell while his friend was gone." The cop pointed to a blood mark on the side of the faux-marble sink. "Must have hit his head as he went down. A piece of the mirror sliced a deep gash in his upper right arm."

The female EMT glanced up at Brody. "The glass cut his artery. He almost bled out. Vitals aren't good. We're transporting him to the military hospital on post."

Brody eyed the head wound. Blunt-force trauma as well as a laceration. Taking out his smart phone, he photographed the pattern of broken glass on the floor, blood spatters on the wall and the injuries to the victim's head and arm.

He also snapped a shot of the bathtub. "Why the filled tub?"

The cop shook his head. "No clue at this point."

The female EMT started to stand. "We need some space."

Brody backed out of the hallway and headed for the kitchen, where Jenkins introduced him to Ted Upton. Ted shrugged off a handshake by holding up his bandaged fingers and explained how he'd been cut.

"How long were you at the hospital?"

"A couple hours." The kid rolled his eyes. "You know how slow emergency rooms can be."

"You went to the hospital on post?"

"That's right."

"How was PFC Webb when you left him?" Brody asked.

"The same as always, laughing and talking about the future. He planned to do some small jobs in the kitchen and then grab some chow from the fridge."

Brody opened the refrigerator. Two store-wrapped sub sandwiches sat untouched. "What time did you get here this morning?"

"Shortly after ten."

"Anyone else stop by?"

The PFC shook his head. "No, sir."

"What did you see when you returned to the house?"

"My sister was on the floor in the bathroom, holding a towel to Josh's arm."

"Did you notice her car parked outside?"

"I thought it belonged to one of the neighbors."

"Do you know the neighbors?"

"Only Nikki Dunn."

Brody raised his eyebrow, waiting for more information.

"She works at the exchange on post." Ted glanced into the living room and watched the EMTs roll the stretcher carrying Josh's unresponsive body out the front door. The policemen hastened behind them.

"Do you recall anything bothering Josh recently?" Brody asked. "Had he argued with anyone?"

Ted shook his head. "Josh does his own thing. We're

friends, and we go back a long way, but he keeps his business to himself."

Stephanie entered the kitchen.

Ted glanced at Major Jenkins. "If you don't mind, sir, I'd like to follow the ambulance to the hospital."

The major patted the soldier's back. "I'll go with you. Give me a minute. I want to speak to your sister."

"Roger that, sir."

Jenkins talked quietly to Stephanie while Brody moved even closer to Ted. "It's a shock to see your friend injured."

The soldier licked his lips. "Yeah, but I've seen worse."

"Your convoy was hit in Afghanistan."

Ted nodded. "That's how Josh lost his legs."

"You were injured, as well."

"Goes with the job, if you know what I mean."

Brody doubted the PFC had worked through the trauma of the IED explosion. More than likely, he was covering up the way he really felt.

Ted dug in his pocket for his keys. "I borrowed my squad leader's car today to help Josh. Tell Major Jenkins I'll be outside in Sergeant McCoy's gray Chevy."

Brody nodded. "Take care of that hand."

"Will do, sir."

He watched the PFC leave the house. Major Jenkins concluded his conversation with Ted's sister and exited through the kitchen.

"Ma'am." Brody approached where she stood. "I'd like to ask you a few questions."

"You're the CID agent."

He nodded. "Brody Goodman. We talked on the phone."

"Thanks for getting here so quickly."

"Can you tell me what you saw when you came into the house?"

She nodded. "The front door was locked. Josh had his iPod tuned to the Braves game. The volume was high. I didn't think he heard me knock."

"How'd you get in?"

"The kitchen door was hanging open. He's on my caseload so I stepped inside and called his name."

"Did he answer you?"

"No." She let out a tiny breath. "The radio was so loud I doubt anyone could have heard me."

"So it was easy for you to enter the house without him knowing?"

Her brow rose. "I don't see what you're getting at."

"The door was open, ma'am, and you came inside unannounced."

"I wasn't trying to do him harm."

Brody raised his hand and smiled apologetically. "I wasn't implying you were, but if someone had wanted to sneak up on Private Webb, they could have."

"They would have found him on the floor. His wheelchair had overturned. He must have hit his head when he fell. Glass cut his arm."

"He was bleeding?"

She nodded. "I grabbed a towel and tried to stop the flow."

"You mentioned calling nine-one-one."

"That's right. Then I phoned his battalion."

"Your brother was in the house at the time?"

"Ted arrived when I was on the phone with you." She glanced out the window at the ambulance before turning her gaze back to Brody.

"Did your brother know you had accepted the AW2 position?" he asked.

"I've only been in Freemont for a couple days, Agent Goodman. My brother and I have been playing phone tag."

"For that long?"

"I really don't see how any of this has bearing on Josh's fall."

"Force of habit for a CID guy, I guess." He smiled. "You found lodging rather quickly."

"My father has a house in town. He's away on business. I'm staying at home until I can find an apartment."

Brody eyed her for a long moment and then asked, "Was the water running in the tub when you arrived?"

She nodded, her eyes somber. "I turned it off before it overflowed."

"What about outside? Did you see anything suspicious when you pulled into the housing area?"

"Not really."

He raised a brow. "Meaning?"

"Meaning a pickup raced out of the subdivision and nearly ran into me just before I turned into the housing area."

"Can you ID the vehicle or the make and model?"

"A red truck. Souped-up. Big knobby mud tires. Lots of chrome."

"Did you see the driver or the license plate?"

"Everything happened too quickly. It was raining. My windshield wipers couldn't keep up with the downpour."

"Which direction were you coming from?"

"I'd visited two of my clients in Freemont and was heading south to meet with Joshua."

The pickup could be some kid's ego ride, but it could also be the vehicle the perpetrator used to race away from the scene of the crime. Either way, Brody would encourage the Freemont police to track down the red truck with big tires.

He glanced outside. The door to the ambulance was closed, and the vehicle pulled out of the driveway escorted by one of the squad cars. The remaining officer reentered the house. Brody excused himself and met the cop in the living room.

"You might want to take a second look at the blood spatters on the bathroom wall." He pointed toward the hallway. "The pattern indicates the PFC's arm was cut when he was still in his wheelchair."

The cop narrowed his gaze. "You're saying he cut himself?"

"Or someone else inflicted the wound. Ms. Upton said the back door was open when she arrived on the scene. Earlier someone raced out of the subdivision. A red pickup with oversize tires. Might be prudent to knock on a few doors in the neighborhood and see if anyone saw the truck or anything suspect this morning. A lot of people have had access to the house, but you could still check for prints."

The officer nodded, and when Stephanie stepped back into the living room, he took out his notebook and pen. "Ma'am, I need to ask you a few more questions."

"What kind of questions, Officer?"

"About the truck and the back door and how you entered PFC Webb's house."

Stephanie bristled.

"He's just trying to determine what happened," Brody volunteered.

"What happened is that Joshua Webb fell from his wheelchair and cut his arm, and if I hadn't arrived when I did, he might have died."

"Your brother was here earlier," Brody said.

Her face clouded. "You think Ted had something to do with Josh's injury?" She shook her head, her eyes wide and eyebrows arched. "That's preposterous."

"Is it? Then you shouldn't object to the questions."

Brody often relied on his gut feelings when investigating a crime, and nothing about the pretty advocate seemed suspect. He was more prone to consider Ted Upton as someone of interest.

Bottom line, no matter what she told the cop or how convinced Brody was that she wasn't involved, he planned to keep his eyes on both Stephanie Upton and her brother.

The police officer's questions were similar to the ones the CID agent had asked Stephanie earlier, except they lacked the accusation she had heard in Brody's voice. The local policeman was thorough, while attempting to make her feel as comfortable as possible, which she appreciated.

Throughout the questioning, Brody stood to the side and watched her with dark eyes that revealed nothing about his own feelings concerning the case. At least six inches taller than her five foot seven, he had deep-set eyes and full lips that failed to smile.

She mentioned phoning Joshua and having her call go to voice mail, which sent Brody on a hunt through the house to uncover the missing cell. He returned to the living area with a smug look on his angular face. "Looks like he retrieved your message."

At the conclusion of the questioning, Stephanie gave both the officer and the CID agent her business card. "You know where to find me if you have any more questions."

She hurried from the house without as much as a backward glance at the special agent. Checking her watch, she let out a frustrated breath at being held up so long. She needed to join her brother and Major Jenkins at the hospital. As the AW2 advocate, her job was to be a liaison between the military and the injured soldier and to help with all his needs, including medical. She was also concerned about Ted and wanted to ensure he was coping with Joshua's accident.

Before she reached her car, a small, two-door sedan pulled to the curb. The driver hustled toward her.

"Ms. Upton?"

She didn't know the man, but she saw the high-tech digital camera in his hand.

"I'm a reporter with the Freemont paper." Without asking her permission, he raised the camera and clicked a series of pictures. "I'd like to interview you for a story about the rescue."

"Rescue?"

"You saved Josh's life. Just like you did three years ago."

Her stomach soured. Surely he didn't plan to resurrect the past.

"I'm not interested in an interview or having my picture in the paper," she insisted, her voice firm.

The shutter clicked again.

Stephanie raised her hand to hide her face. "Please!"

"You heard the lady."

She turned to find the special agent charging along the sidewalk to where the reporter stood.

"No interviews. No pictures. Is that understood?"

The newsman hesitated.

Brody stepped closer. His eyes narrowed and his lips clamped together in a downward frown.

"Got it." The reporter took a step back. "Not a problem. I'm outta here." He scurried to his car and raced from the subdivision.

Brody touched her arm. "Are you okay?"

She nodded. "I'm fine, but thanks for the help."

"The reporter mentioned a previous rescue. You mind telling me what he was referencing?"

"It has nothing to do with today."

Brody stared down at her with questioning eyes.

She sighed, knowing he wouldn't give up until she told him what had happened in the past. "If you must know, a storm came up on a nearby lake and caught Josh and my brother and a few of their friends unprepared. I arrived in time to pull some of the kids from the water."

"Some?"

"One of the boys—my cousin, Hayden—drowned."

"I'm sorry."

"So am I."

He continued to stare at her. "Are you sure you're okay?"

She nodded decisively. "I'm positive. Now, if you'll excuse me, I have a soldier on my caseload that may need help at the hospital."

Frustrated with the mix of emotion bubbling up within her, Stephanie climbed into her car. She hadn't wanted to talk about the accident on the lake, but Brody seemed to have pulled the information from her.

She regretted her defensiveness, which he must have recognized. In truth, she wanted to know what had happened to Josh as much as Brody did. Just so he realized she and Ted weren't at fault.

Maybe her brother had been right.

Maybe she shouldn't have come back to Freemont.

TWO

Stephanie parked her Corolla next to the Fort Rickman Hospital's emergency room and hurried inside. The clerk at the desk directed her to the intensive-care unit. She rode the elevator to the third floor and followed the signs to the ICU, where she checked to ensure Josh's hospital-entrance forms had been properly filled out.

Satisfied his paperwork was complete, she continued on to the ICU waiting room, where she found Ted sitting on a vinyl couch with his elbows on his knees. He looked younger than his twenty-one years and so very vulnerable.

He glanced up when she entered the room.

"Any news yet?" she asked, wanting to put her arms around him and draw him close.

He shook his head. The glare in his eyes warned her against any display of affection.

Major Jenkins stood nearby. "The doctor ordered three units of blood. The nurse said they won't know anything for a number of hours. His parents are with him now."

With a deep sigh, Ted stood and walked toward the large window. He stared down at the parking lot below, as if trying to hide the worry that was plastered over his pale face. "The…the nurse said everything was being done to save his life."

"I'm sure he's getting the best of care." Stephanie knew the struggle her brother was waging to remain in control. "Joshua is a fighter, Ted. He'll pull through."

"Dad said Mom was a fighter, and you know what happened to her."

"That was different."

He turned, his face tight with emotion. "Different because she had cancer or different because you weren't around to watch her life waste away?"

Stephanie's breath hitched. She hadn't expected the bitterness she heard in his voice.

Working to keep her own voice calm, she said, "Mom wanted me to finish the semester at college, but I came home every weekend."

"Which wasn't enough."

How many times would he need to hear the truth before he could accept what happened? Her mother regretted not having the opportunity to get a degree and had insisted Stephanie continue her studies.

A freshman in high school, Ted had needed someone in his life. That someone should have been their dad, but he'd buried his own pain in his job. Stephanie had tried to fill the void on the weekends when she came home, never realizing it wasn't enough for Ted. Worried though she was about Joshua's condition, she was even more worried about her brother.

Footsteps sounded in the hallway. She turned, expecting to see Joshua's physician. Instead, she saw Brody Goodman.

He hesitated in the doorway, glancing first at her and then at Ted, who stared out the window. "Did something happen?"

"The doctor's with Josh now," she said, hugging herself. "He's critical and receiving blood."

Ted's cell trilled. He pulled the phone to his ear and nodded. "You heard right. Josh was admitted to ICU. Third floor. The waiting room is at the end of the hallway."

He disconnected. "Paul Massey's downstairs. He's home on leave with orders for Fort Hood and heard about the accident." Ted glanced at the major. "Paul stopped by Josh's house, sir. One of the neighbors mentioned seeing an ambulance."

Stephanie was surprised by the change in Paul when he joined them in the waiting room. Previously a gawky kid with big eyes and long hair, the soldier who greeted Ted was tall and tan and sure of himself.

"Hey, man, what's going on?" Paul asked as he and Ted gripped hands.

"The doc said they'll know more after he's transfused. They won't let anyone back there except his parents."

As the soldiers talked, Brody and the major stepped into the hallway. Stephanie couldn't hear what they were saying, but she was convinced it had something to do with the CID agent's suspicions about Josh's injury.

The major nodded and glanced at her ever so briefly, his expression difficult to decipher. Brody waved a hand in the air and then paused. His eyes locked on hers for a long moment.

Her cheeks burned.

Averting her gaze, Stephanie smiled at Paul, who gave her a warm hug.

"Glad you're back in town, Steph."

"She took over as the AW2 advocate." Ted's tone was anything but enthusiastic.

Paul nodded with approval. "You'll be good at that job."

If only. Seemed her brother would be her biggest challenge. Right now, she didn't feel up to the task.

She glanced at her watch. "I need to get back to work, Ted. I'll call you later."

He fiddled with his phone. "Whatever."

"Sorry to interrupt." Stepping into the hallway, she looked first at the CID agent and then at Major Jenkins. "I need to change clothes before I make another house call."

"Why don't you take the rest of the afternoon off?" the major suggested. "You still have to get settled, and the Hail and Farewell starts at four o'clock."

Jenkins turned to Brody. "I saw your name on the list of folks being welcomed to post."

"Glad you reminded me. After three weeks, I feel like an old-timer." Brody tilted his head and smiled at Stephanie. "So I'll see you there?"

"Probably."

She didn't want to go to the social event, but it was

a command performance. After the new people on post were welcomed, she planned to hurry back to her father's house.

Not that she wanted to be there, either. Too many memories remained of her mother and the way life had been before cancer took her life. The change in Ted after her death, coupled with their father's detachment, had added to Stephanie's grief.

The problems had culminated that night on the lake.

A night that had changed her life forever.

A night she never wanted to think about, yet coming back to Freemont threatened to put it front and center once again.

After talking to Major Jenkins, Brody returned to CID headquarters and headed for the chief's office.

He knocked and then pushed the door open. "Sir, do you have a minute?"

"What do you need, Brody?"

Wilson was big in stature, with a short buzz of black hair and equally dark eyes set in a round mocha face. He glanced up from the open manila folder as Brody approached his desk.

"An incident involving one of our injured soldiers." Brody relayed the information about Josh's accident.

"You think it was intentional?" the commander asked.

"Yes, sir. Due to the blood spatter. The woman who found the victim is the new AW2 advocate. Her brother was with the victim earlier in the day. He injured his hand and went to the hospital for stitches. While he was gone, Webb was attacked."

"Seems a bit coincidental."

"Yes, sir. He and Webb are both assigned to the Warrior Transitional Battalion. PFC Upton seems to have a short fuse, especially when it comes to his sister."

Wilson nodded. "Sounds like a problem waiting to explode. The Freemont police are handling the investigation?"

"Currently they're in charge, although their first assessment missed the mark."

Wilson's full lips twitched. A spark of amusement glimmered in his brown eyes. "I presume you set them straight."

"I pointed out the obvious, sir. All with deference to their position as lead investigators on the case."

"How'd you learn of Webb's injuries?"

Brody explained about the call to Joshua's battalion. "I was in Major Jenkins's office at the time. He was called away from his desk for a few minutes and asked me to man his phone."

"That was fortunate. You were discussing your interest in PTSD?"

"Yes, sir. Major Jenkins agreed to let me speak to the battalion. They've received support from other on-post agencies, but I want to make sure they're aware the CID could provide additional resources."

Wilson leaned back in his chair. His right hand tapped a mechanical pencil against a tablet on his desk. "What you experienced was regrettable, Brody.

I applaud you for turning tragedy into something positive for other military personnel."

"That's my hope, sir."

"Seems you've arrived at Rickman at the right time. The post commanding general is concerned about the growing number of violent shootings around the country. A handful of veterans have been involved. The media seems to focus on their tie-in with the military, which paints all of us in a bad light. General Cameron is insistent that we remain proactive at Fort Rickman and defuse any problems before they get out of hand, especially when redeployed soldiers are involved. I realize the local police are investigating, but I want you involved, too. Keep your eye on the advocate, as well as her brother. Family troubles can escalate in a heartbeat."

"Yes, sir, but isn't the CID short staffed at this time?"

"As is the entire army." Wilson pointed to a folder on the corner of his desk. "We have two new special agents transferring here within the next few months, which will resolve our manpower problems. Until you hear otherwise from me, follow up on this current case. Take as much time as you need. I'll know where to find you."

"Yes, sir."

"Keep me posted on Webb's condition. Be sure to let the Freemont police know of our interest in their investigation."

"Yes, sir."

"Tact is important when working with local law

enforcement. We've had a fairly good relationship in the past. I wouldn't want that to change."

"I agree, sir."

"They've got a new chief of police. Name's Don Palmer. I'll call him and mention your interest in the case."

"Thank you, sir."

Wilson shifted forward, a visible sign the discussion was over. "I'll see you at the club this afternoon."

"Four o'clock. I'll be there, sir."

Returning to his desk, Brody logged on to the internet and pulled up the local newspaper's home page. He wanted to learn as much as he could about the Upton family, and the local rag would, no doubt, provide information.

Tapping into the archives, he searched for stories on Stephanie Upton. A number of articles popped up.

Brody shook his head in amazement.

Stephanie's accomplishments ranged from swim team to prom queen. The pictures showed a teen with sparkling eyes, shoulder-length hair and an inviting smile.

His own high school in California had four times as many students as Freemont High. He'd played sports and had his own fair share of news mentions, but nothing compared to the hometown darling who was also dubbed Girl Most Likely to Succeed.

On a more solemn note, he uncovered an obituary for a Jane Upton. "Survived by husband, Davis, daughter Stephanie and son Theodore." Brody did the math. Ted had been a freshman in high school. Stephanie must have been in college. "Memorial donations can be made to the American Cancer Society." All too well, Brody knew the toll malignancy took on families. His maternal grandfather had died of colon cancer, a disease that with proper screening could have been prevented.

Stephanie had mentioned her father was out of town on business. He entered the dad's name in the search box and clicked on an article that recapped the elder Upton's success growing his company into a large enterprise that provided jobs for many folks in the local area.

Mr. Upton's picture showed a tall man with a receding hairline and twenty extra pounds tucked around his middle. Davis Upton appeared to be an older and heavier version of his son.

Returning to the archives, Brody found a story on the drowning incident at the nearby lake—Lake Claims Local Teen.

He opened the file and quickly read about the group of teens who had partied on Big Island Lake shortly after their graduation. As Stephanie had mentioned, the frivolity turned deadly when a storm hit unannounced. The teens were caught in the rapid currents on the straits that ran between Big Island and Small Island to the south. Stephanie had boated to the island and pulled the teens to safety. All except Hayden Allen, a cousin on her mother's side.

Brody leaned in closer and read Keith Allen's comment on Stephanie's attempt to save his brother.

"My mother and I appreciate Stephanie's heroic

efforts to find Hayden. Without regard for her own safety, she searched tirelessly for my brother, for which we are grateful."

A team of divers eventually found the missing teen's body tangled in debris.

Brody saved the article to his hard drive as well as his smart phone and then inserted a printed copy into a manila folder labeled Investigation: PFC Joshua Webb.

On a hunch, he dialed Major Jenkins.

"It's Brody, sir. I've got a question for you."

"Shoot."

"You said Joshua Webb and Ted Upton enlisted at the same time. Do you have the date they entered the military?"

"Not at my fingertips, but I'll call you back."

According to the article, the two PFCs, along with Paul Massey, had been part of the group of teens at the island. The tragedy happened three years ago on June 10, just twelve days after the group had graduated high school.

Brody wrote the names on a clean sheet of paper and added Stephanie's at the bottom. Next to hers, he drew a large question mark.

His phone rang. "Special Agent Goodman."

"I found the information, Brody." Jenkins's voice.

"Yes, sir."

"Both Webb and Upton enlisted three years ago, on the thirtieth of June."

Twenty days after Hayden's death. Fast-forward to a deployment in Afghanistan and an IED explosion that injured both soldiers.

Brody picked up the printout of the article. On the bottom of the page was a photo of Stephanie Upton. The girl named Most Likely to Succeed had failed to save her cousin.

The expression she wore revealed deep emotional pain and a tragic sense of loss. Hayden's brother had offered praise for her attempts, but the slant of her eyes and heavy pull on her shoulders told a different story.

All too often what happened in the past had bearing on the present. Stephanie could have suffered as much trauma as her brother had in Afghanistan and still be fighting her own internal battles. If so, she might not be the best person to help Fort Rickman's wounded warriors.

No law enforcement officer worth his badge believed in coincidence. Nor did Brody. The Upton siblings had some history with a dead relative and a group of friends who had joined the military, perhaps to distance themselves from the lake tragedy.

Call it a long shot, but Brody wondered if that history played into what had happened to Joshua Webb. If so, he needed to uncover the truth about the struggle between Stephanie Upton and her brother. At this point, neither person was a suspect, yet Brody had to be open to any possibility. In the days ahead, he planned to keep his eyes and his attention focused on both of them.

He would talk to Major Jenkins about Ted, but he'd keep his concern about the AW2 advocate to himself. He was more intrigued than suspicious about her involvement, but either way, she needed to be watched. Wilson had given Brody an assignment, one he was determined to fulfill.

THREE

On her way to the Fort Rickman Club later that afternoon, Stephanie drove past the large brick quarters that surrounded the main parade field. So many families had lived in the homes since they had been built in the 1930s. Growing up, she'd known a few "Post Toastees," as the locals called the army brats, but she'd always associated with kids from Freemont. Now she regretted her own attempt to isolate herself from the military. She'd been young and too focused on herself.

Her mother's illness and Ted's troubles during high school had changed her outlook on life. Not that her family hadn't had their share of problems before her mom had gotten sick. After her death, everything had been exacerbated by a workaholic father who preferred to stay at the office rather than deal with the situation at home.

Evidently, her father still hadn't changed. Case in point, his current trip to Europe, supposedly to oversee the start-up of a satellite company. To his credit, he had visited Ted often at Fort Sam and had provided for additional specialists to consult with the military docs, yet he handled Ted as if he was a business venture instead of his needy son.

Over the past few years, Ted had rejected Stephanie's outreach so many times that she had finally decided their relationship could never be reconciled. Then the job had opened at Fort Rickman, and she'd transferred home.

If she believed in God's intervention, she would be convinced He had stepped in. As it was, she had severed her relationship with the Lord three years ago.

Refusing to spend any more time focused on the past, she turned into the lot for the Fort Rickman Club and found one of the few remaining parking spots in the last row, farthest from the brick facility. Hot air wrapped around her as she climbed from the car. Beads of sweat had dampened her brow by the time she entered the club, causing her to shiver in the cool, air-conditioned interior.

She rubbed her arms in an attempt to stave off the chill, as well as her own nervousness at having to make small talk with people she didn't know. Hopefully, as soon as the introductions were over, she could slip out unnoticed.

First thing tomorrow morning, she planned to see Joshua, if he was allowed visitors by then. The last word from the hospital was that his condition remained critical.

A swarm of military and civilian personnel filled the club's main ballroom. Threading her way into their midst, she stretched on tiptoe and searched for Major

Jenkins and any of the other people with whom she now worked.

"Stephanie?"

She turned to find Special Agent Goodman standing behind her. His dark eyes, which had been elusive earlier, now flashed with warmth.

"I didn't think I'd ever find you in this crowd."

He'd been looking for her?

To cover her surprise, she glanced quickly around the ballroom. "Everyone on post must be here."

He pointed to a table set up in the corner and raised his voice to be heard over a group of young officers clustered nearby. "I was on my way to grab a cold drink. May I get you something?"

"A bottle of water would be great."

Brody leaned closer to be heard over the surrounding chatter. A subtle hint of aftershave wafted past her—a masculine scent that caused a tingle of interest to play along her neck.

"Do you mind coming with me? I don't want to lose you in the crowd."

She hesitated for a fraction of a second before his hand touched the small of her back. He guided her across the room. A number of folks smiled. Others nodded in passing.

At one point, Brody halted her forward progression in order for a distinguished couple to pass. The man was dressed in the army's digital-camouflage uniform. Two stars were attached to the center front tab.

"That's General Cameron, the post commanding general, and his wife." Brody's lips hovered close to her ear. "They're nice folks. He's a by-the-book type of guy who puts his soldiers first. Mrs. Cameron is a charming Southern belle who treats everyone with sincerity and warmth."

A younger couple waved and then headed toward them. The guy—dressed in a sport coat and tie, just as Brody was—slapped Brody's shoulder in greeting and turned to Stephanie, his eyes twinkling with mirth. "Don't believe anything this guy tells you."

The attractive woman at his side smiled. "I'm Michele Steele, and the CID agent giving Brody a hard time is my husband, Jamison."

"Nice to meet you both."

"Stephanie's the new AW2 advocate," Brody told them.

"An important position." Jamison's smile was encouraging. "It's good to have you on board."

"Jamison and I work together," Brody told her. "Michele is Colonel and Mrs. Logan's daughter." He pointed to the older couple talking with the commanding general and his wife. "Her parents are as nice as she is."

"You and Stephanie need to come over for dinner." Michele looked at her husband, who nodded in agreement. "Jamison could throw some steaks on the grill."

Grateful though Stephanie was for the invitation, she wasn't sure socializing with the special agent was a good idea, especially after the pointed questions he had voiced earlier.

After chatting for a few more minutes, she excused

herself to look for Major Jenkins and spotted him standing near the stage.

"The general will call your name shortly," he said as she approached. "I provided him with information he'll mention when he introduces you. All you'll have to do is shake his hand and smile."

Stephanie adjusted her skirt and tucked her hair behind her ear, a bit on edge at the thought of being introduced, especially knowing Brody was in the crowd.

When her name was called, she joined the general on the raised platform and smiled at the sea of faces and military uniforms. In the distance, she spied Brody. His eyes held her gaze for a long moment, causing a flush of heat to work along her neck.

The general recounted the previous job she had held at Fort Stewart and praised her background in social services. She appreciated the information Major Jenkins had provided.

"I know our injured soldiers will find the support they need with Ms. Upton filling the AW2 advocate position."

"Thank you, sir." After shaking the general's hand, she hurried offstage.

Relieved to have the introduction behind her, Stephanie said goodbye to the major and headed for the door. Before reaching the exit, she heard Brody's name announced. Turning back, she watched the ease with which he climbed the platform and stood next to the general.

The post commander praised his accomplishments and valor during four deployments to the Middle East.

A number of men and women in uniform cheered when his time in combat was mentioned. As the next name was called, Stephanie left the club and hurried across the parking lot.

Nearing her car, she groaned. The left rear tire was flat as a pancake. What else could go wrong today?

Her brother's hateful comments at Josh's house came to mind. What better way to prove his point than to put obstacles in her path?

He wouldn't have hurt Josh, but deflating her tire wasn't outside the realm of possibilities. As a teen, Ted had gotten into trouble for doing exactly the same thing.

Tears of frustration and aggravation burned her eyes. In addition, she felt betrayed.

Retrieving her cell from her purse, she called his number. More than anything, she wanted to stop the downward spiral of their relationship before things got completely out of hand. When he failed to answer, she disconnected instead of leaving a message. What she had to say should probably be done in person.

Plus, she needed to focus on the current problem. Namely her flat tire. How hard could it be to put on the spare?

Her moment of optimism plummeted when she opened the trunk and stared down at the numerous parts of a jack she didn't know how to assemble.

Brody Goodman had come to her aid with the newspaper reporter, but recalling the effect his aftershave had had on her earlier, she didn't want to get too close to him again. Even if she had to call a cab, she was better off having nothing to do with the CID agent. As far as she was concerned, Brody was the last person she should ask for help.

Chief Wilson motioned to Brody after he left the stage. "The provost marshal is here, along with some of his people who have been on a temporary assignment in D.C. He wants you to meet them."

The commander of the Military Police Department on post was personable and talkative. He introduced Brody to the returning members of his staff. By the time Brody edged out of the group, Stephanie was nowhere to be found.

Frustrated, he left the club and headed to his car, surprised to see her in the distance, staring into her open trunk.

As he neared, she glanced up. "I seem to have a problem." Which was evident by her clutched hands and wrinkled brow.

Bending down, he examined her tire. "I don't see any big gashes in the rubber. Smaller holes are often difficult to find."

"I ran over some gravel on the way to the club."

"That shouldn't have been a problem, unless a nail or some other sharp object became embedded in the rubber. A mechanic would be able to tell."

He unscrewed the cap on the air valve and whistled. "I found the problem. The valve core's been removed. It regulates the flow of air in and out of the tire. No wonder it's flat."

Standing, he brushed off his hands. "I'll put on your

spare, but that's a short-term fix. You'll need to stop by a tire dealer in the morning."

"Could the valve have jostled loose when I was driving?"

"Hardly. The core was intentionally removed." He pulled out his phone. "We'd better notify the military police."

She shook her head. "I don't want the MPs involved."

"Because—"

"Because I'm new on post. A solider on my caseload was injured this afternoon. I've stirred up enough problems for one day."

He didn't understand her logic. "Someone vandalized your property, Stephanie."

"But—"

They both turned at the sound of a car. Paul Massey was at the wheel of a metallic-blue Dodge Dart with Ted next to him in the passenger seat. A woman sat in the rear, a small blonde who waved when the car braked to a stop.

"Need some help?" Paul asked as he stepped to the pavement.

Brody shook his head. "Thanks, but I can handle it."

Stephanie frowned as her brother rounded the car. "Haven't you done enough for one day, Ted?"

His neutral expression soured. "What's that supposed to mean?"

"My tire's flat. Someone tampered with the air valve. Does that bring anything to mind?"

Before he could reply, the backseat blonde exited the car and scooted next to Ted. "Hey, Stephanie."

"How are you, Nikki?"

"Bummed about Joshua. Ted said you saved his life."

"I merely called nine-one-one. Luckily the paramedics arrived in time."

Nikki Dunn. Brody recalled the girl's name. "Don't you live in Joshua's housing area?"

"That's right. Just down the street."

"I'm Special Agent Brody Goodman with the Criminal Investigation Division. Ted mentioned you today. Were you at home this morning?"

"Until eight-thirty when I left for work."

"Did you see anyone hanging around the area?"

"A couple of neighbors heading into town."

"Any strange cars?"

She shook her head.

"What about a red pickup with jumbo tires?" Brody's gaze flicked between the three twenty-somethings. "Know anyone with that kind of ride?"

Ted's eyes narrowed. He glared at his sister.

"No one in my area." Nikki seemed oblivious to the tension between the two siblings.

Paul glanced at his watch. "If you're okay with the tire, I'll take Ted back to his barracks."

"Any chance you guys drove by here earlier today?" Brody asked rubbing his jaw.

"We've been at the PX since three." Ted tapped his foot against the pavement.

"Playing with the iPads in the entertainment section," Nikki added. "They were waiting until I got off work. We went for pizza after that."

"At the Italian Parlor? How many of the free peanuts did you eat?" Stephanie stared at her brother.

Nikki patted Ted's arm and smiled. "I told him he had to be careful, especially since you and your mom were both allergic."

"Yeah, but as Stephanie knows, I take after my dad on that count." He turned and motioned to Paul. "We better get going."

"I heard Ted's angry comments earlier today over the phone." Brody stepped closer to Stephanie as Paul's car left the lot. "Seems he doesn't know how to deal with the IED explosion and his injuries so he's taking it out on you."

"That's not true."

"Isn't it? You're protecting your brother because you love him, but that's not helping him heal."

"Having the MPs question Ted won't help, either."

"Did he vandalize tires as a kid?"

When she didn't respond, he took a step closer and looked into her troubled eyes. "I can call the local police to find out, or you can tell me and make it easier on both of us."

She pulled in a fragile breath. "My mother died of cancer when Ted was in high school. He had a hard time dealing with her death and got into trouble."

"Tampering with air valves," Brody filled in. "You think he did this today?"

"I don't know what to think." She wrapped her arms around her waist and looked both vulnerable and needy.

Brody wanted to put his arm around her shoulder

to offer support, but he doubted Stephanie would approve of the gesture. Instead, he reached for the jack. "After I change your tire, I'll follow you home. In the morning, I can arrange to drive you to work while your tire is being repaired."

"That's not necessary."

"Maybe not, but it's the least I can do under the circumstances. Besides, how do you plan to get to work tomorrow?"

She tried to smile. "Okay. I'll accept your offer, but you don't have to worry about my relationship with my brother. We'll get through this one way or another."

Brody's heart went out to Stephanie. More than anything, he wanted to tell her everything would be okay, but if Ted had tampered with her tire, his aggression could escalate to something worse. Add Joshua's attack to the mix and Ted became a serious threat.

Stephanie thought her family's problem could be resolved—and maybe things between them would eventually straighten out with professional help for her brother. In the interim, Brody wanted her to be safe instead of sorry. He'd keep investigating the case, but he would also ensure nothing happened to Stephanie.

FOUR

Brody kept Stephanie's car in sight as she drove through town and then eased onto a narrow two-lane street that wove through the countryside. The road eventually led to a large brick entryway with a stucco sign that read Country Club Estates.

She turned into the upscale community with Brody close behind. They drove past a number of homes ablaze with floodlights that illuminated the massive structures and sleek construction. Huge picture windows offered views into the expansive interiors and multilevel living spaces.

Brody had grown up in a modest ranch smaller than the pool houses showcased in floodlights at the rear of a number of the vast properties. Hopefully, the wealthy provided loving environments for their own families amongst the lavish trappings of their success. Supposedly God loved the poor, but the poor often didn't love their own. Case in point, his father.

Stephanie pulled into the driveway of a brick house with a wide front porch, white trim and wrought-iron gaslights that should have been turned on. Instead, the house sat dark and shadowed and made Brody thankful he had accompanied her home.

He glanced around the well-manicured front yard as he stepped from the car. "Nice digs."

Flicking his gaze to the rear of the property, he looked for anything that might cause problems. Brody noted the fairway and green, edged by dense woods that sat about fifty yards from the rear of the structure. "I didn't know Freemont had a golf course."

"It's off the beaten path, which is what the developer wanted when he proposed the area. My parents were some of the first folks who built here. The newer homes are more elaborate. My dad opted for comfortable and easy to maintain."

Comfortable was an understatement. Brody walked Stephanie up the stairs to the porch and reached for the keys she held in her hand.

"Allow me."

Although he couldn't see her expression in the darkness, he heard the slight intake of air. Maybe she wasn't used to men who opened doors for her. The thought brought a smile to his lips that quickly vanished when the door swung open.

"Didn't you lock your door?"

"I…I thought I did." She raked her hand through her hair. "I came home to change and was in a hurry to get back to post for the Hail and Farewell."

She started to enter the house.

With his hand on her arm, he held her back. "Let me check everything first."

He stepped into the darkened interior and pulled

back the edge of his jacket. His fingers touched the leather holster that held his service revolver, just in case.

The croak of tree frogs and buzz of cicadas filtered through the open door. His eyes adjusted to the darkness, revealing plush furniture and large palladium windows. A patio and swimming pool were visible beyond the deck in the backyard.

Moonlight filtered through the windows and provided enough light to guide his steps as he moved from the dining room past the butler's pantry to the huge kitchen with eat-in breakfast nook and keeping room. At the far end of the house, he found a master bedroom and bath with walk-in closets that were larger than the living room in his bachelor officer's quarters on post. Another hallway led to a pair of smaller bedrooms and adjoining baths.

With meticulous thoroughness, Brody checked the many nooks and crannies in the home where someone could be lying in wait. Once he was assured that the first floor was empty, he flicked on the lights and circled back through the rooms.

A stone fireplace graced one side of the expansive main room, flanked by two full-size couches and a collection of maritime memorabilia. The nautical theme continued into the hallway where a collection of watercolors of naval vessels decorated the walls.

Opening the door to the three-car garage, he saw a late-model Cadillac and a BMW convertible and let out a long whistle in appreciation of her father's good taste in cars.

Satisfied that at least the first floor was secure, Brody returned to the front door and held it open. "Everything looks okay on this floor, but I still need to check the upper floor and basement."

Stephanie tilted her head and tapped her foot. "Does that mean I can come inside now?"

He smiled at her impatience. "Sure, but wait at the door while I check the other floors. It shouldn't take long."

True to his word, Brody returned a few minutes later. He found Stephanie in the kitchen. Her demeanor had changed. She appeared shaken and totally focused on a photograph lying on the counter.

His neck prickled when he gazed down at the five-by-seven glossy of a group of four teenage boys. A red bull's-eye had been drawn with some type of marker around the head of one of the guys and superimposed with a large X.

"It's Josh." Stephanie's voice was shaky as she focused on the face behind the markings. She pointed to a sheet of typing paper lying nearby—"Why did you come back to Freemont?"

Brody read the typed message and then glanced back at the photo. "I recognize Paul and your brother. Who's the other kid?"

"Hayden Allen. My cousin who drowned. This was the last picture taken of the four guys together." Her voice caught. "Ted kept the photograph on the bulletin board in his room."

"He must have come home today and typed the note and marked the photo."

"It wasn't Ted." She shook her head. "He never would have done this."

"Surely he has a key to the house."

"I presume he does, but—"

"If Ted didn't do it, then someone else entered your house and desecrated the photograph. He, or she, left a threatening note. Either way, I need to inform the local police."

"No, Brody." She grabbed his arm as he pulled his cell phone from his pocket. "I don't want them involved."

Because of Ted.

Once again, Stephanie was protecting her brother, yet Ted was the most likely suspect. He undoubtedly had a key to the house and, from what Brody had overheard today, was upset with his sister.

Either in anger or distress, the PFC had marked the photo and typed the message. Was he warning Stephanie someone else would be hurt if she didn't leave town? Or was he telling her the next person in the bull's-eye might be her?

Stephanie pulled in an anxious breath. The bull's-eye didn't make sense. Ted and Josh had been friends since elementary school. Surely what had happened in Afghanistan hadn't altered their relationship, yet someone wanted to scare her into leaving Freemont.

The nerve endings on her arm tingled and confirmed the effectiveness of the warning. The front door hadn't been locked when Brody tried the key, although she had engaged the dead bolt when she left for post. At least she thought she had.

Just as Brody implied, her brother was the only other person with access to the house.

"Stephanie?"

Brody was staring at her with his dark eyes. She heard the question in his voice that said more than just her name. He, too, realized the significance of the picture and typed message.

Stepping toward the sliding glass door that opened onto the deck, she flipped the wall switch that turned on the recessed lights in and around the pool.

An antique maritime bell hung at the edge of the landscaped area. One of her father's treasures from the past and a reminder of the night her mother had died. Stephanie could still see Ted, a skinny and gaunt high school freshman, standing in the dark night, ringing the bell over and over again. Probably to get their father's attention, but their dad had been too involved with his own grief to worry about his children.

Brody moved beside her. Even without looking, she knew he was searching the yard and golf course beyond. No doubt searching for some sign of Ted.

"Your brother comes home often?" His question sounded more like a statement.

"I'm not sure." Turning away from Brody, she reached for the photo.

He grabbed her hand. "Not so fast. I need to check the picture for prints."

"You'll find Ted's. I told you the photo belongs to him."

Brody continued to grip her hand as if he feared she'd ignore his request. Drawn to the controlled strength of his hold, she glanced up once again, finding his gaze intense. There was something under the surface that Brody wasn't willing to share, something more than his concern for an injured soldier. In that fleeting moment, she glimpsed an unspoken need. For what, she wasn't sure.

A flash of awareness passed between them. He pulled in a breath and released her hand.

The separation jarred her. Surely she hadn't wanted him to continue touching her. Or had she?

Surprised and angered when tears pooled in her eyes, she blinked them back. What was it about this man that caused such a mix of emotion to well up within her?

She didn't need someone to protect her. She needed someone to tell her how to heal the deep, destructive rift with her brother.

Not that Brody could help. He made everything worse. Or so it seemed. In fact, he was the least likely person to help her heal the past—both her own and her brother's.

Ignoring the connection that had passed between them, Brody pointed to the typed text on the note. "Look at the words *you* and *come* and *to Freemont*."

She leaned closer. "The *o* is smeared in each case."

"That's right. It's not crisp like the other letters. I saw a computer and printer in your father's office."

Stephanie followed Brody to the downstairs level and into the home office. Her father's nautical collectibles lined the bookshelves. A ship's wheel hung on the wall next to a brass porthole cover and a large print of a battle on the high seas.

The only nonmaritime item was a picture of her with Ted and their mother. The perfect family. At least that's what most people thought.

Brody turned on the computer and the printer. "Do you know your father's password?"

She typed in the code. When the screen opened, she stepped back to give Brody room. His strong hands played over the keyboard.

He typed, "Why did you come back to Freemont?" The words appeared on the monitor. He hit Print. A mechanical hum filled the silence. A sheet of paper rolled onto the printer tray.

They both gazed down at the typed message. Each letter was crisp and clear without a hint of a smudge, including the *o*.

Relief swept over her. "I told you it wasn't Ted."

"The only thing we can rule out is that he didn't use this printer. I'll check the ones at the Warrior Transitional Battalion tomorrow and the adjoining barracks where your brother lives. The library on post probably has computers, as well."

"Are you going to tell Ted what happened?" she asked.

"I'll ask him if he came home recently and whether he has a key to the house."

"This is his home, Brody. He has every right to come and go as he pleases."

He let out a frustrated breath. "A man was injured today, Stephanie. I need to find out who did it and why. Your brother's actions could play into that investigation. I'm especially interested in learning why he doesn't want you around. Is there anything you haven't told me?"

"You're making more of this than it warrants. Brothers and sisters don't always get along. Our relationship has nothing to do with Josh's accident."

From the determination she saw on Brody's face, she knew he wasn't accepting what she had to say.

"Change your locks, Stephanie. You've got a security alarm system. Be sure to use it, and don't let your brother into the house."

He dug in his pocket and handed her his business card. "Program my phone number into your cell. Call me if you feel threatened in any way."

Brody's nearness caused heat to warm her neck. She raised her hand to cover her flushed skin. She didn't want the CID agent to realize the way she reacted to his closeness and his questions. As appealing as he was in one way, the accusation she read in his penetrating gaze brought a very different type of reaction—one she didn't like—to tingle along her spine.

"I'll keep your phone number close by, Brody, but I'm sure I won't need to call you."

"Then I'll see you in the morning. Any idea what time the mechanic will be on duty?"

"Walt prides himself on opening by seven o'clock. He even includes it in his advertisements."

"I'll be outside your house at six forty-five. You can leave your car at the garage and I'll give you a ride to work. Unless you want to drive the Caddy or BMW."

In spite of what he thought about Ted, she appreciated Brody's thoughtfulness. She didn't want to be beholden to her father, and driving his cars would do exactly that. "I'll take you up on the ride."

Returning to the kitchen, Brody placed the picture and printed note in a plastic bag she provided and tucked it carefully in his jacket pocket.

Together, they walked into the foyer. At the door, he turned too quickly, leaving her a breath away from his broad shoulders.

"Remember, lock your doors and turn on the alarm. If your brother shows up, call me. No matter what time." Brody leaned closer, his gaze intense. "Do you understand me, Stephanie? Call anytime. My phone will be on."

She squared her shoulders, willing herself to be unaffected by his nearness. "I'll be fine, Brody."

Before she could say anything else, he was out the door. She hesitated, evidently a moment too long, because it opened once again.

"Turn on the alarm and lock the door." His voice was firm. "I'm not leaving until you do both things."

She made a shooing motion with her hand. Once he stepped back onto the porch, she closed the door and turned the lock, feeling somewhat satisfied as she twisted the dead bolt and heard the resounding click when it slipped into place.

Stepping toward the security-alarm panel, she tapped in the code. The warning lights flashed, and a beep confirmed the system was engaged.

Brody's footfalls sounded down the porch steps.

She pulled back the curtain in the living room window and watched him climb into his car. The engine engaged.

Even in the darkness, she saw him turn and stare at the house. His eyes flashed in the night. Or was her mind playing tricks on her again?

The headlights came on, illuminating the road as he pulled away from the curb.

With a heavy sigh, she turned from the window and gazed into the massive entryway and living area beyond.

Why did you come back to Freemont? The words of warning flashed through her mind.

Pulling her cell phone from her purse, she tapped in Ted's number and sighed with frustration when it went to voice mail. "It's Stephanie. Call me. I'm at home."

Hanging up, she headed to her childhood bedroom, overcome with a sense of déjà vu. If only her mother hadn't died, everything would still be good, the way she wanted her life to be.

Despite the warning, she wouldn't run away from Freemont. She'd done that once. So had Ted. Now they were both back, and this time she wouldn't let him down.

She flipped on her bedroom light. As keyed up as she was, she'd need to read to calm her frayed nerves before she tried to sleep. She hadn't eaten, but food was the last thing on her mind. Maybe she'd make a sandwich later.

In the bathroom, she scrubbed her face and changed into her nightgown, feeling a bit more refreshed.

Glancing at the books on the shelf near her bed, she reached for an anthology of short stories her mother had given her. Finding comfort from the well-worn volume, she grabbed the corner of the plush comforter and pulled back the covers, eager to crawl into bed and lose herself in one of the stories she loved to read.

Glancing down, she moaned.

Tears clouded her eyes. Her heart skittered in her chest and her shoulders tightened.

As much as she wanted to run away, she couldn't pull her gaze from the bull's-eye that marked her bottom sheet. Superimposed over it was a large red X, just like the one that had covered Joshua's face in the photo.

A typed note was pinned to the pillowcase. "Leave Freemont or you'll be in the bull's-eye."

Her brother would never do something so hateful.

Yet, if Ted wasn't playing a terrible joke on her, then who had been in her house and what was the real meaning of the bloodred markings?

FIVE

A sense of foreboding settled over Brody when he drove away from Stephanie's home. Glancing back, he had seen her at the window, staring into the night. He hadn't made any points with her this evening, but then his job wasn't to impress her. He needed to convince her to be cautious and to realize her brother's struggle could lead to more problems.

Tomorrow he would talk to her about changing the locks as well as the code on the security alarm, even if she didn't think either precaution was necessary. More often than not, folks outside law enforcement failed to realize the need to be proactive when it came to their own safety. Couldn't she see these threats were personal?

Turning left at the next intersection, Brody drove through the upscale community, focusing on the thick patches of underbrush as well as the shadows behind cars and around fences, searching for anything suspect.

He passed two other vehicles on the road as he canvassed the area, getting to know the layout of the terrain. Although everything seemed in order, someone could be hiding in the darkness. A man on foot could easily pass from house to house and never be seen under the cover of night.

Was Ted Upton in the local area, or had he returned to the barracks? Brody reached for his cell and tapped in the executive officer's number. Major Jenkins answered on the fifth ring.

"Hey, sir. It's Special Agent Brody Goodman. Sorry to bother you after duty hours."

"Not a problem."

"I wanted to determine PFC Upton's whereabouts. Could you notify the duty sergeant and ask him to check Upton's room?"

"Do you mind telling me why you're concerned? Has there been a problem?"

"His sister had an unwanted visitor earlier this evening, which could have been Upton."

"Was she harmed?"

"Negative, but I want to ensure her brother remains on post tonight, and I'd appreciate your help."

"You've got it, of course. I'll have one of the sergeants stop by Upton's room and keep an eye on him."

"I appreciate it, sir."

"Anything else I should know?"

"Only that Ms. Upton may be late for work tomorrow. She had a flat tire and needs to see a mechanic in the morning."

"Why am I thinking it's strange you're the one providing that information?"

"Just trying to help. She'll probably call you in the morning. I'm giving you a heads-up."

"Good enough. I'll contact the WTB."

Wanting to check the Upton property one more time, Brody retraced his route. The night seemed as placid as the water in Stephanie's backyard pool, until he turned onto her street and saw the lights blazing from every room in her house.

His neck tingled a warning. He reached for his cell and tapped in her number. Each ring seemed to last an eternity. His gut tightened. He pulled to the curb, ready to throw the phone on the console, leap from his car and race toward her house with his weapon drawn.

She answered with a cautious "Hello?"

"It's Brody."

He jerked the car door open and stepped onto the pavement. "I'm standing outside, Stephanie. You've got every light on. Are you all right?"

"Yes, of course. I'm fine."

She sounded mildly vexed at him for calling. Whether she liked it or not, he wouldn't leave until she provided a logical answer to the light issue.

"Do you have a problem with the dark?" He couldn't hide the concern in his voice.

"Meaning what, Brody?"

Meaning why didn't she give him a satisfactory answer?

"Electricity costs money, Stephanie. I'm just wondering why every light is on."

He could hear her sigh over the phone. "I was checking the house, just as you did earlier."

His heart softened. He'd scared her, which he hadn't wanted to do. She needed to be cautious, but not fearful.

"You want me to hang around for a while?"

She laughed. The sound lightened the moment. "Thanks for the offer, but I'm feeling better now."

"Why don't you reassure me by opening the front door?"

"Once again, you're being overly protective."

"Humor me, okay?"

She let out another sigh. "I've already changed for bed."

"Then wave from the window."

"If you insist." Her tone had warmed.

The curtain in the dining room moved and Stephanie appeared, backlit. She raised her hand and waved.

"You're okay?" He pulled the cell closer to his lips and stepped toward the window where she stood.

She turned ever so slightly. The light played over her face, allowing him to see her upturned mouth and nodding head.

"I'm okay, Brody. Besides, it's time for me to call it a night. You should go home now."

"Your door's still locked?"

"Of course."

"And the alarm's on?"

"Exactly as it has been ever since you left thirty minutes ago."

"I checked your house, Stephanie. You're locked in. I drove through the neighborhood, as well. Everything seems secure, but if you hear anything outside, call me."

"I'll be fine tonight."

"Then I'll see you in the morning."

He disconnected and headed back to his car. As he climbed behind the wheel, he shook his head. Stephanie probably thought he was crazy for hanging around, but he felt better knowing she was okay.

Glancing back, he watched the lights flick off one by one. The backyard was dark, but the floodlights on the front porch and upper deck remained lit, which would be a deterrent if anyone were wandering around in the night.

Plus, Stephanie had the alarm.

Slowly, he turned onto the main road and drove back to Fort Rickman. Once on post, he headed to his office and checked the photo for prints, finding none, which meant the glossy finish had been wiped clean. He'd have someone go over the note in the morning.

Returning to his car, he drove to the local fast-food restaurant on post and picked up a burger with fries, supersized, and a cold drink.

Usually he would have been anxious to get home, but with the questions that circulated through his head about Stephanie Upton and her estrangement with her brother, Brody doubted he would get a good night's sleep. Instead, he would probably stay up late, pretending to watch the sports channel, while he tried to put together the pieces of this investigation.

What was it about Stephanie Upton that bothered

him? He sighed. *Bothered* wasn't the right word. She'd gotten under his skin. He didn't know how or why.

He hadn't been attracted to anyone since Lisa and had never thought those types of feelings would surface again. Yet here he was thinking about a woman who was totally focused on repairing her relationship with her brother, a man Brody considered a threat.

Once inside his quarters, he shoved the burger and fries into his mouth and gulped down the cola. His mixed emotions might have been brought on by hunger, but even after eating, he couldn't get Stephanie off his mind.

Talk about a conflict of interests. Maybe he should turn over the investigation to someone else at headquarters and move on. He shook his head, knowing that wasn't an option, especially as short staffed as they were. Besides, something had happened to him today. Whether appropriate or not, he was already involved.

Stephanie exhaled, deeply confused by Brody. Why had he been hanging around her house? Surely it had nothing to do with her and everything to do with Ted. She never should have allowed the special agent to follow her home or to come inside.

She hadn't told him about the markings on the bedsheets, fearing he would instantly suspect Ted. If his attitude toward her brother changed, she would show him the note that had been pinned to her pillowcase. Taking care not to touch her hand to the paper, she had used tweezers to enclose the message in a Ziploc bag, just as Brody had done with the note in the kitchen. He could run a fingerprint check later, when and if she told him about the incident. For now, she would keep the information to herself.

After turning off the lights, she headed for the guest room, knowing she'd never be able to get any rest in her own room with the marked bedding. Once again, she tried unsuccessfully to call Ted.

Tomorrow, she would track him down and have a heart-to-heart talk.

Would he listen?

More than likely, he'd fiddle with his smart phone and check his email, maybe send a text message or two to indicate that he wasn't interested in healing their relationship or in anything she had to say. She'd already gotten that message with her unreturned phone calls and his hateful comments at Joshua's house earlier today.

Regrettably, Brody had heard those comments, too. If only she could erase what had happened and start fresh.

But it was too late for that.

Brody would be back bright and early the next morning. She needed to get some sleep, but when she turned off the light, she saw Joshua's face and the blood on the bathroom floor.

She tossed and turned for what seemed like hours until she finally drifted into a fitful slumber, studded with horrific dreams. She was in the water, swimming through murky blackness. The wind howled around her, hurling large whitecaps that crashed over her head.

A deadly cold soaked into her bones along with a heavy lethargy, yet she had to go on.

Diving down into the turbid water, she reached for Hayden. His hand slipped from hers, replaced with a flash of memory. Something she'd buried from her youth in the deep recesses of her psyche.

The flash disappeared.

She was on *The Upton Queen,* her father's boat. Ted stood at the stern, his hand gripping the rope attached to the ship's bell. Over and over again, he yanked on the cord, causing the bell to peal into the night.

She could see it play out with dreamlike clarity.

Nikki leaned against the railing, a large beach towel around her shoulders, staring with big eyes into the lake. Paul and Josh sat on the deck, impaired by the alcohol they had consumed. Another teen, Cindy Ferrol, appeared too pasty white, her shoulder injured from jumping off the rope swing into the rapid current. Tears streamed down her blotched cheeks.

The bell continued to peal.

Stephanie tried to drown out the death knell that sounded too loud, too real, too—

She sat up in bed, a cold sweat dampening her neck.

The bell hadn't been a dream.

As she listened, it tolled again. Once, twice, three times.

The chilling sound filled the night and sent her scurrying down the hallway and into the great room. She stepped to the window and peered out at the dark pool and the yard beyond, expecting to see Ted.

Instead, she saw the water and the trees and the now-silent bell.

Was her mind playing tricks on her?

Or was someone out there? She thought of the photo of the old gang and the bull's-eye covering Joshua's face. Nikki, Cindy, Paul? They had heard Ted ring the bell. Were they trying to scare her tonight? Or were they all in danger?

Stephanie had made a mistake three years ago. She couldn't make another mistake. The stakes were too high.

Today Josh had been injured and could have died.

Next time, would it be Ted? Or Paul?

If only she could remember what she had seen that night as she searched for Hayden. A flash from her past that eluded her even now.

A sound on the front steps caused her to turn from the window and stare through the foyer at the oak door. Had it been a creaking porch floorboard or footsteps?

She held her breath, listening. All she heard was her pounding heart mixed with the drone of the air-conditioning system and the hum of cool air coming through the vents.

Glancing down, she realized her cell phone was in her hand. She had programmed Brody Goodman's cell number into her contacts file. As much as she wanted to call him, she couldn't feed his growing antagonism toward her brother.

The security alarm was on. The doors and windows

were locked. Earlier, Brody had assured her she was safe. Nothing had changed, except now she didn't feel safe or secure. Was she in danger?

SIX

The front door opened the next morning before Brody had climbed the stairs to the Uptons' porch. Stephanie stood in the threshold, wearing a flowered top and flowing skirt and a smile that sent a warm glow to his midsection. An unexpected breeze picked at her skirt and swirled the thin, gauzy cotton around her legs. The motion of the material drew his eyes to her strappy sandals and pink toenail polish.

The collar of his white shirt felt tight. He adjusted his tie and pulled his gaze away from her toes and back to her eyes, which were regarding him with a hint of mischief, as if she realized the effect the pink polish had on him.

Attractive though she was, and as cute as her toes were with the flashy polish, Brody had to admit he was even more taken by her attempt to be upbeat after everything that had happened yesterday.

"Give me a second to set the alarm and then I'll be ready," she said. The system beeped as she tapped in the activation code. A longer buzz indicated the program was set.

Grabbing her purse and briefcase off a small table in the foyer, she stepped outside. "Something tells me you didn't grow up in a small town." She pulled the door shut behind her.

"Only if you call L.A. small."

She laughed, a throaty sound that caused a curl of interest to tighten his chest. "Here's how it works in Freemont. We may have home security alarms, but we rarely use them."

He gave her a mock salute. "Then thank you, ma'am, for humoring me today by arming and activating your system."

"I wouldn't want you to worry." She laughed again, but as close as they were standing, Brody could see the tiny lines of fatigue that pulled at the corners of her smile. Evidently, she had slept as little as he had.

"Ferrol's Garage is on one of the side streets downtown," she said as they walked toward her car.

Brody pointed to the rear tire. "That spare doesn't look very dependable, Stephanie. I'll be right behind you if there's a problem."

He held the door and inhaled the sweet floral scent of her perfume as she slipped past him into the driver's seat. Once she buckled up, Brody climbed into his own car. Stephanie drove at a modest speed, and they reached Ferrol's Garage's parking lot without incident.

The door to the mechanic's bay hung open. A man in jeans and a gray short-sleeved shirt peered out from under the hood of a car.

"Long time, no see, Stephanie." He walked outside to greet them, wiping his hands on a small towel that was shoved in his back pocket. "I heard you were staying at your dad's place."

"Until I can find an apartment." She introduced Brody, who shook the mechanic's strong, work-worn hand.

Walt Ferrol was about five-eleven and stocky, with a thick neck and beady eyes that narrowed even more when he glanced at Brody's gray slacks and light-weight sport coat.

"You must be a civilian."

"Actually, I'm a warrant officer and special agent with the Criminal Investigation Division. We wear civilian clothes when investigating a case."

The mechanic's face tightened. "Don't tell me you're here because of what happened to Joshua?"

"Are you aware of anyone who would want to harm Private Webb?"

"Not Josh. He was always a good kid. Shame what happened to him in Afghanistan."

"What about a red pickup with oversize tires? Anyone you know own that type of vehicle?"

Walt whistled, long and low. "Sounds like that juiced-up Ford Hayden Allen used to drive."

Stephanie shook her head. "It was raining, and the visibility wasn't good, but I never thought it was Hayden's truck."

"What happened to the Ford?" Brody asked.

"You'd have to talk to Keith," Walt said.

Brody remembered the name from the newspaper story. "Hayden's brother?"

Stephanie nodded. "That's right."

"Keith has an office at Freemont Real Estate," the mechanic volunteered. "He started working for them right before the influx of new military folks came to town. Made a killing, or so folks said."

Brody raised his eyebrow ever so slightly at the mechanic's choice of words.

Walt tugged at his chin. "How does Hayden's Ford tie in with what happened to Joshua?"

"It wasn't Hayden's truck," she insisted.

"Stephanie saw a red pickup with mud tires leaving Josh's subdivision right before she discovered his injuries," Brody said, watching how Walt processed the information.

The mechanic hesitated a moment, and then leaned toward her. "Did you recognize the driver?"

She shook her head. "Everything happened too fast."

Walt sniffed. "Probably just a coincidence, then."

Brody pulled a business card from his coat pocket and handed it to the mechanic. "Call me if you hear anything that might have bearing on this case. I want to know who's responsible."

Walt nodded enthusiastically. "I feel the same way. Especially since Josh and Cindy were such good friends."

"Who's Cindy?" Another name from the newspaper article, but he would let Walt tell him what he already suspected.

"My baby sister. She and Josh went to school together." He pointed to Stephanie. "Along with her brother, Ted, and Hayden and Paul Massey and Nikki

Dunn. They were inseparable, but after Hayden's death, the whole gang fell apart."

Shaking his head at Stephanie, he added, "My sister rarely sees Nikki, yet the two girls were so close in high school."

"People grow up and grow apart, Walt."

He pursed his full lips. "I suppose you're right. Cindy works for me in the office now. Helps out in the shop if we're busy. She's got herself a little place east of town. A few acres."

"Good for her."

Walt pointed to Stephanie's Corolla. "Looks like you could use a new tire on that back wheel."

"That's why I'm here." She opened the trunk and stepped back so Walt could inspect the flat tire. "There's a problem with the valve stem."

The mechanic chuckled. "What happened? Ted playing tricks again?"

She bristled. "Of course not."

He rubbed his fingers over the worn rubber tread. "Don't like being the bearer of bad news, but the tread's about gone on this baby. Doubt it would last to the end of the week, even with a new valve stem."

Brody agreed. "Is there a tire dealer in town?"

Walt jammed a thumb back at his own chest. Pride flashed from his eyes. "You're looking at him. If you want, I'll order you a new tire, Stephanie. Should take a couple days. Although if you want my advice, I'd replace all four tires. To be safe."

She groaned internally. Her monthly budget was

already stretched too thin. "I'll have to think it over. Get a quote. Then call me."

She pulled a business card from her purse and scribbled another number on the back before handing it to Walt. "My cell number's listed under my name. The landline to my office is on the other side."

A late-model sports car pulled into the lot. The driver, a woman, early twenties with brown hair, waved. She wore tight jeans and a gray polo that matched Walt's shirt.

Big silver loops dangled from her ears, and a number of bracelets clinked as she walked toward them. "Hey there, Stephanie. I heard you were back in town. Ted must be glad to see you."

Ignoring the comment about her brother, Stephanie introduced Brody to Walt's sister, Cindy.

"How are you, ma'am?"

"A few minutes late this morning. Is there anything you need, Walt?"

"Check the price on new tires for Stephanie's car."

"Will do."

Walt gave Stephanie's card to his sister and pointed to Brody. "Special Agent Goodman asked about Hayden's truck. Someone driving a similar vehicle may have been involved in Joshua's accident."

Cindy shook her head. "I haven't seen his truck around these parts for at least two years. Keith would know for sure." She glanced at her watch. "He opens his office at eight, but he usually eats breakfast at the diner. You might find him there."

Once back in his car, Brody turned to Stephanie and smiled. "I'll buy breakfast."

"You don't need to talk to Keith. The truck wasn't Hayden's."

"You're sure?"

She sighed. "I told you, everything happened rather quickly. All I saw was a red pickup with oversize wheels that screeched out of the subdivision. I was more concerned about not getting hit rather than the make and model, yet it didn't seem as big and bulky as Hayden's truck."

Brody glanced at his watch. "No pressure, but we've got some time before work and I'm hungry. If we see Keith, so much the better."

With a look of resignation, she pointed to the next intersection. "Turn right on Third Street. The diner's not far from the courthouse on the square."

Brody headed toward the center of town. "From what Walt said, I gather Cindy and Ted were friends in high school."

Stephanie nodded. "All the kids hung around together. Ted and Nikki dated most of their senior year. They broke up, and she ended up going to the prom with Hayden."

"In his spruced-up red Ford?"

Stephanie smiled. "Which all the girls loved. Hayden was a ladies' man as well as a good kid."

"Walt said the group fell apart after his death."

"The guys enlisted. Cindy used to help her mom with a home-cleaning business. I'm not sure when she started working for Walt. At some point Nikki got a job at the PX on post."

"How did she take Hayden's death?"

"Nikki was devastated. All the kids were. Folks in town mourned his death, as well. Hayden had been accepted to Georgia Tech and planned to be an engineer like his dad. People thought he'd come back to Freemont and help to put the town on the map."

"So his death was tough on everyone."

Stephanie nodded. "Especially his mother. Hayden was Aunt Hazel's pride and joy. Her marriage wasn't the best, and my uncle died when Hayden was in middle school, which is probably why she clung so tightly to him. He was definitely her favorite."

"She's your mother's sister?"

"That's right."

"Tell me about Keith. Growing up, were you two close?"

She tilted her head. "Keith was two years older than me and had his own friends."

"What about his relationship with Hayden?"

"There was a bit of sibling rivalry, which happens in a lot of families. Hayden excelled in just about everything he did. Folks thought he would go far."

"And Keith wasn't the shining star?"

"He didn't have the spark that made Hayden stand out. Everyone liked Hayden, and my aunt made no attempt to hide which son had her heart."

"Was Keith jealous of his brother?"

"Not that I could tell."

"How's his relationship with his mother now?"

"I'm not sure. Aunt Hazel suffered a stroke not long after Hayden's death. Keith couldn't care for her at home and placed her in the local nursing home."

A sad situation all around.

The diner appeared in the distance. Brody parked in the lot behind the small restaurant. Stephanie nodded to a number of the early-morning patrons, who smiled as they entered. A waitress pointed them toward a booth and brought two cups of steaming coffee along with menus.

"How's the food here?" Brody asked once they were seated and the waitress had retreated to the counter.

Stephanie glanced at him over the menu. "Home cooking and very Southern."

"Which means grits and biscuits and gravy are a must." Brody's mouth watered.

Before he could motion the waitress back to the table to place their order, a man stepped inside. Early thirties with slicked-back hair. He was wearing a light blue, button-down collared shirt and khaki slacks and stopped to talk to a number of the diners before he spied Stephanie and waved.

Her shoulders tightened and the tendons stood out on her slender neck as he approached their table.

"How are you, Steph?"

"Fine, Keith."

He shoved a hand in Brody's face. "Keith Allen. Walt said you're from the fort."

Brody stood and accepted Keith's outstretched hand. "Special Agent Goodman, with the CID."

"Investigating what happened yesterday." Keith shook his head with regret. "I hated to hear that Josh was hurt."

"Walt phoned you?" Brody asked.

"He wanted to make sure I met up with my favorite cousin." Keith smiled down at Stephanie, still sitting in the booth. "Mother asked about you. She heard you came home."

"How is Aunt Hazel?"

"The same. No better. No worse." He turned to the waitress and held up his hand. "Coffee, Charlotte."

She poured a cup and headed his way. "You want a menu, Keith?"

"Not today. Bring me the usual."

"You joining these folks?" the waitress asked.

Stephanie glanced at her watch. "I wish we could stay, but I've got to be at work soon."

So much for Southern cooking and a hot breakfast. Brody followed Stephanie's lead and dropped a handful of bills on the table. "Coffee's all we have time for this morning, Charlotte."

Stephanie slid from the booth. "Brody's looking for a red pickup with big tires. Walt told him it sounded like Hayden's Ford, but you got rid of the truck some time ago, right?"

Keith nodded. "I sold it at Old Man Lear's car auction a few months after Hayden's funeral."

"Who made the purchase?" Brody asked.

"A farmer from Alabama, but I can't remember his name. I've probably got it at home someplace. Does it have bearing on what happened to Josh?"

"Not necessarily. Do you know anyone who would want to do Josh harm?"

Keith shook his head. "Not in this town. Folks are interested in giving him a hand up. I've got a group of business folks who want to cover his home-remodeling expenses." He glanced at Stephanie. "We can talk about those plans once Josh's condition improves."

"I know he could use the help," she said.

Brody handed his card to the real-estate agent. "If you find the farmer's name, call me."

"Good seeing you, Keith." Stephanie turned to leave.

"Wait, Steph." He grabbed her arm. "I heard you were the new AW2 advocate on post. I was working with the guy who held the position before you. We planned a picnic for some of the soldiers in the WTB a week from Saturday. Did you happen to see the file in his office?" Keith shrugged and smiled sheepishly. "I guess it's your office now."

"I looked it over briefly. I…I didn't realize you were coordinating the event."

He held up his hand. "I'm just one of many folks interested in supporting our military. We've got lots of corporate sponsors. It should be a great day. I rounded up the old gang and asked them to get involved."

"The old gang?"

He nodded. "That's right. Paul took leave so he could help. Nikki's volunteered, and Cindy, too. I wanted everything to be special for Ted and Joshua. Of course, after what happened yesterday, I don't know if Joshua will be able to attend."

"Did you get Major Jenkins's approval?" Stephanie asked.

Keith nodded. "He's behind it one hundred percent."

"A week from Saturday doesn't leave much planning time."

"Not to worry." Keith smiled. "Everything's on schedule—in fact, a few of us are meeting today to check out the facilities. Why don't you join us? Two o'clock at the marina, or we can meet up on the island if you want to take your dad's boat. The city recently renovated the picnic facilities and they're top-of-the-line."

"I'll check my schedule and get back to you." Once again she glanced at her watch and then at Brody as if needing his help. "I've got to go or I'll be late for work."

Brody followed her outside. Something was going on between Keith and Stephanie, an undercurrent Brody couldn't explain. Every family had its own secrets, although in small towns secrets were often hard to keep.

He thought of the note left on Stephanie's kitchen counter. Had someone other than Ted warned her away from Freemont?

"You mind explaining what the problem is with you and Keith?" he asked once they were in his car.

"There's no problem."

"Come on, Stephanie. I could feel the tension between you two."

"It's nothing that's relevant to your investigation, Brody."

He glanced at her for a long moment before he pulled onto the road. "We're going back to your house."

"Why?"

"So you can get a change of clothes and some better shoes if we're going to the island later today."

"We?"

"I'll drive you. Besides, I told Major Jenkins I wanted to help the WTB."

She glanced at her watch. "I don't want to be late for work."

"You won't be. I promise."

But when he drove into the Country Club Estates and turned onto Stephanie's street, Brody's gut tightened, knowing he wouldn't be able to keep his word.

"What happened?" Stephanie's eyes were wide as she stared at her house.

A police car was parked on the curb. Two officers stood on her front porch, staring into her windows, their guns drawn.

Stephanie opened the passenger door before Brody had put the car in Park. He grabbed her arm. "Stay in the car."

"It could be Ted. I need to know what happened."

"Let me check it out first." Before she could object, he had rounded the car and closed the passenger door. The air-conditioning was running, and the cool air from the vent brushed against her hair but did nothing to calm the anxiety that rolled through her stomach.

She opened her door again and stepped onto the sidewalk, determined to hear what Brody was saying as he approached the officers and held up his CID identification.

The car engine muffled their voices so she caught only snippets of conversation.

"…the alarm…"

"…locked…checked the rear…"

Brody nodded and walked back to where she stood.

"Did something happen to my brother?" she asked, half-afraid to hear his response.

"The security alarm went off. The police responded, but the doors are locked. Give me your keys and we'll check the house."

"Did they say how it happened?"

"Only that sometimes the motion sensors can be activated if there's a pet inside. Even dust in the system can be a problem."

She shook her head. "No pets."

"Wait here."

The three men disappeared into the house. She caught glimpses of them through the windows as they fanned out to various areas of the two-floor structure.

In a shorter time than she had expected, Brody appeared in the doorway, his face somber. He motioned her forward.

Anxiety tingled along her spine. She knew full well

what he had found. Something she hadn't mentioned either last night or this morning.

"We found a bull's-eye on your bedsheets." His voice was tense but controlled as she climbed the steps.

"I know, Brody. The marks and the note were there yesterday. That's the reason I had the lights on last night."

"But you didn't tell me?"

"I didn't want to alarm you."

He clenched his hands for a moment and then relaxed them as he gently took her arm and ushered her inside.

The two police officers were in her bedroom. "They're getting prints," Brody explained. "The sheets will be taken in as evidence."

"Nothing happened to me last night."

"Someone marked your bedding, Stephanie. He, she or they left a warning. That's not something to laugh about."

"I'm not laughing."

"But you failed to tell me."

She straightened her spine. "Because you would have suspected Ted."

"Do you think he's responsible?"

"Absolutely not."

"Who else would come into your home and desecrate your bedding? Is there something from your past? Maybe something that happened after Hayden's death? Someone that wants you out of town?"

She shook her head, suddenly seeing everything through Brody's eyes. "I should have told you."

"What about your job at Fort Stewart? Is there anyone who might follow you here and try to do you harm?"

"Not that I'm aware of."

"Anyone who was confrontational?"

"Never."

"Where did you find the typed note?"

"Pinned to the pillowcase. I used tweezers to put it in the plastic bag."

"Then you did plan to give it to me?"

She sighed. "I don't know what I planned to do."

"Is there anything else I don't know, Stephanie?"

"The bell." She glanced through the large windows and pointed to the backyard. "I awoke in the night and thought I heard it ringing, but when I went to the window no one was there."

"What time was that?"

"After midnight."

"Anything else?"

"A sound on the front porch. It was probably the wind."

"You said probably. If it wasn't the wind, what else could it have been?"

"It sounded like footsteps."

His eyes widened ever so slightly. "But you didn't call me."

She shook her head. "The alarm was on. The doors were locked. You told me I was safe."

His voice softened. "I told you to call me."

She turned away, unwilling to see the disappointment in his gaze. In hindsight, she had made a mistake by not calling him. Last night, her only thought had been to protect Ted. This morning she realized how vulnerable she had been.

Someone had entered the house.

To scare her?

Or to do her harm?

SEVEN

The Freemont police gathered evidence and checked the front door for prints before they left. Stephanie packed a small tote with an outfit and shoes appropriate for the trip to Big Island and met Brody back in the living room.

"I really am sorry," she said. "A lot happened yesterday. I've been worried about my brother. The shock of finding Joshua. All the blood." She tried to smile, knowing she wasn't successful. Surely he recognized her struggle.

"I wasn't thinking straight," she continued to explain. "Plus, we had only just met yesterday, and calling in the middle of the night didn't seem right. If I had felt threatened, I would have dialed nine-one-one. You can see from the officer's response today, help would have arrived."

He nodded. "I don't want you to be unduly afraid, but the bull's-eye on your sheets was significant. You've got to be cautious and aware of your surroundings at all times."

"I understand."

"You also need to change your locks and your alarm."

"It's my father's house. I don't have that authority."

"You could call him."

"I could, but I don't think it's necessary at this time."

Brody shook his head as if exasperated by her response. "At least promise that if anything else happens, you'll call me. That's why I gave you my number."

"I will."

"Now, let's get you to work."

She walked with him to his car, relieved they had reached an agreement of sorts. He seemed less certain that Ted was involved and more concerned that someone else could have entered the house. Why had she left the door unlocked yesterday? Or had it been locked, as she'd originally thought?

Sitting next to him in the passenger seat, she turned to look out the window as he headed for Freemont Road, which led to post.

At least everything was out in the open now, and she would call Brody if there was a next time, which hopefully there wouldn't be. Surely what had happened yesterday was a once-in-a-lifetime occurrence. If only she knew what had triggered the anger someone must harbor against her or her family.

Her dad had made enemies in his years running a large company. Some folks had been laid off. Others were upset about his expansion in Europe and questioned why he didn't grow his United States assets. With the downturn in the economy, she was sure he had a number of disgruntled employees. Perhaps the attack had been aimed at him.

She sighed inwardly, knowing the warning had been for her. Her sheets had been marked, and the note had been pinned to her pillowcase.

Paul and Hayden had been close prior to their senior year. After Hayden's death, Paul had turned to Ted for support and had followed both Josh and her brother into the army. She'd heard talk that he had wanted to be deployed along with his buddies and regretted his stateside assignments.

Ted blamed her for what had happened to Hayden. Did Paul, as well?

She turned toward Brody, his steady gaze on the road, his lips downturned. Lips she didn't want to look at now.

He was probably mentally going over what had happened, just as she had been. His left hand gripped the steering wheel. The other one rested on the console, so very close to hers.

Too close.

She wiggled toward the door. Everything about Brody had become a huge distraction.

She swallowed hard. The air-conditioning blew on her face. She adjusted the vent.

"Are you too cold?" he asked.

"A little." She rubbed her hands over her arms.

Brody adjusted the thermostat. "Better?"

"Yes, thanks." She needed something to focus on instead of Brody's penetrating eyes, which seemed to look into her soul.

"I'm surprised Keith is involved with the Wounded Warriors," she finally said. "He didn't have much good to say about the army when he was younger."

Brody nodded. "Some kids are drawn to the military. Others aren't."

"The old Keith wouldn't have thought about Josh or Ted. Nor would he have called the gang together and gotten them involved."

When Brody failed to comment, she pursed her lips and shrugged. "Maybe he's changed for the better." She fiddled with her hair and added, "I worried about Keith after the drowning. He was in denial, pretending to be fine, but he had to hurt as much, if not more than anyone else." She dropped her hand to her lap. "You can't lose someone in your family and not be overwhelmed with pain."

Brody nodded.

"Families are important," she continued. "They provide affirmation and support and love."

"Did Keith feel loved by his mom?"

"I'm sure he did, even if she doted on Hayden. Maybe that's why Keith was reserved as a kid. He didn't want to compete with his brother."

"Everyone needs love and affirmation, but people grow up and become stable adults in spite of dysfunctional families and the mistakes they made in their youth." Brody smiled. "I made some poor decisions when I was a kid."

"I'm sure you never messed with someone else's life."

"Mistakes happen, Stephanie."

"Some mistakes are worse than others."

He glanced at her. "Who are we talking about?"

She let out a frustration sigh. "Why, Keith, of course."

"What mistake did he make?"

"Not being there for Hayden."

"Maybe he had to work so hard to protect himself that he didn't realize Hayden needed help, too."

Stephanie thought back to that day on the lake. Keith had been delayed in Atlanta and had failed to pick the teens up from the island. Surely that memory haunted him still, yet he'd never told her why he'd been held up.

"Did you know about the picnic for the Warriors?" Brody asked.

"I saw something on the appointment calendar and glanced at some notes the former advocate had made. The only sponsor mentioned was Freemont Real Estate. I didn't tie it to Keith."

"Sounds like it could be a nice day. Especially if Keith has the WTB commander's approval."

"Maybe, but Big Island isn't the best place for a picnic. It's in the middle of a large lake, and storms come up quickly. We'll have to check that the weather is going to be clear that day."

"I'd be happy to stop by city hall and find out about the facilities before I pick you up this afternoon."

"That would help reassure me. Thank you, Brody."

She sat back in the seat and tried to relax. "You're probably right. The day should be lovely, and I'm sure everyone will be safe."

She wouldn't tell Brody the main problem was that

she never wanted to go back to Big Island. Too many memories still haunted her.

If she felt that way, Ted would, as well. He didn't need anything else to upset him. Especially memories neither of them had been able to forget.

After dropping Stephanie off at her office, Brody talked to her brother's squad leader. Ted had been in his barracks last night, according to the sergeant. Brody didn't know whether to feel relieved or even more concerned.

He called Fort Stewart CID and asked them to question the WTB there, and also the folks who had worked with Stephanie, in case she hadn't realized a danger that someone else may have suspected.

Stopping by his office, he called the Freemont Police Department and set up an appointment to talk to the new chief. Don Palmer, a big guy—midforties—with broad shoulders and a thick neck, greeted him a short while later with a firm handshake.

"My men told me you pointed out a few flaws in their investigation at PFC Webb's house yesterday." He motioned Brody to sit while he poured two cups of coffee. "Appreciate the help."

"Not a problem, sir." Brody accepted one of the cups. The two men discussed Josh's injury and Brody's suspicions. The chief said his men had gone door-to-door in the neighborhood, but no one had seen anything or anyone. In addition, they'd checked for prints but hadn't found anything conclusive.

Brody shared the photos of the bathroom he'd taken

on his phone and discussed the angle of the blood spatter and Josh's head trauma.

"I agree with your assessment," the chief said. "Looks like someone attacked him from behind. Any idea about the bathwater?"

"Not at this point. Although I'll question the other soldiers in the Warrior Transitional Battalion where Josh is assigned and let you know if I hear anything."

Chief Palmer nodded. "I'd appreciate any help you can give us. If you work the on-post angle, we'll investigate in Freemont. Two more set of eyes and ears would be a win-win in my opinion."

"I'll be happy to help."

Brody mentioned the bull's-eyes and notes left at Stephanie's home, hoping the chief might be able to shed light on the vandalism.

"If her door wasn't locked, anyone could have entered the house," the chief said, pointing out the obvious.

"She thought she had engaged the lock, but admitted being in a hurry." Brody shrugged. "New job, rushing to get to post for a social event."

"I'll increase patrols in the Estates."

"Have there been any break-ins?"

"Not recently, but things can change in a heartbeat."

Which Brody knew too well. "I met Keith Allen this morning. He works for Freemont Real Estate."

Palmer nodded. "Keith's a nice guy who does a lot of good in town."

"What about his past?"

"Past as in his youth?"

"If you've got information."

"I grew up in Freemont. The Allen family has always been prominent, although we came from different sides of town. My family was from a less affluent area."

"The Allens were well-to-do."

"*Wealthy* would be a better choice of words. They lived in the Country Club Estates. His father started the development, and his home was the first one constructed in the area."

"So Daddy was in real estate."

"A contractor, who died of a heart attack much too young. His marriage was rocky, and most folks said he worked himself to death. He built many of the buildings in town, as well. Plus, he won a number of bids at Fort Rickman."

"What about Davis Upton? Isn't he a manufacturer?"

"Who also received a number of federal contracts."

"Did the two men work together?"

Palmer shrugged. "I'm not sure, but they both had dealings with new construction on post."

"And both benefited from those jobs."

"That's right." The chief straightened in his chair. "I'm in favor of a man making a living, Agent Goodman, so I don't understand your point."

"Just trying to see the dynamic between the two families. Mrs. Upton and Mrs. Allen were sisters."

"That's right, but the families weren't particularly close." Palmer took a long swig from his cup. "Jane Upton was about six months' pregnant with Ted when

Hazel Allen became pregnant. Up until then, the two families had mingled socially. After the boys were born, some type of split developed, and the two women were rarely seen together after that. About the same time, the Allens' marriage went south."

Brody raised his brow.

The chief shrugged nonchalantly. "A lot of folks are related in a small town like Freemont. Sometimes we like our kin. Sometimes we don't, but they're still kin."

"Tell me about Keith growing up."

"He was a quiet kid. Didn't apply himself to his studies. The same could be said for a lot of high school boys."

"And his brother, Hayden?"

Palmer nodded. "Now I see where you're headed. Hayden was the golden boy who could do no wrong. Everyone in town liked the kid, even though he started running with a wild crowd in his senior year."

"Ted Upton?"

"That's right. They were in the same grade at school, although Hayden was a bit younger. Paul Massey was part of the group. Joshua Webb, as well. The guys were determined to push the envelope in most things they attempted. Two girls hung around with them, Nikki Dunn and Cindy Ferrol. Not that the girls were bad, but they made poor choices in the guys they dated."

"Nikki dated Hayden?"

"She was sweet on Ted at first. They broke up their senior year. Not long after that, she started dating Hayden and went with him to the prom, which seemed to surprise everyone."

"How'd Ted take it?"

"He got stopped for drag racing later that same night."

Brody sat back in the chair. "All this happened three years ago, yet you seem to be pretty sure about your details, Chief. I don't want to be disrespectful, but you mind telling me how you can recall everything with such clarity?"

"My daughter was in Ted's class. For whatever reason, girls like bad boys. I wanted to know everything there was to learn about Ted Upton, and you can bet I kept my eyes on him. Last thing I wanted was to find him with my daughter."

"Did anything develop between them?"

"I didn't let it. In fact, I insisted she head to college for summer semester right after high school graduation. Getting her out of town was the best decision I've ever made. Didn't take her long to realize there were a lot more eligible guys at the University of Georgia, in Athens, rather than back in Freemont, Georgia."

"What about Ted's drag-racing charge?"

"His father got it dropped. Ted enlisted. Josh and Paul followed suit, and life became a whole lot easier once the boys left town."

"They were a constant problem?"

"More like a bigger-than-normal nuisance. Ted came from an okay family, although his daddy was more interested in growing his business than forming a relationship with his teenage son. The mother was a nice lady, liked by all. Shame was, she got cancer and died when Ted was a freshman in high school. The kid went downhill from then on."

"What about his sister?"

"Stephanie tried to keep him on the straight and narrow, but the job was more than she could handle. Ted had a surly mouth and a bad attitude and didn't listen to her. Most folks thought Stephanie did more than she should have to help the kid. With her dad gone most of the time, she reconnected with her aunt Hazel, but that relationship eventually ended."

Brody leaned forward ever so slightly, waiting for more information.

The cop pursed his lips. "You've probably heard about the drowning at Big Island Lake?"

"Bits and pieces."

"Ted, Hayden, Josh and Paul had spent the day on the island. They were drinking. Nikki and Cindy joined them at some point. There used to be a rope swing that swung out over the rocky channel between Big Island and Little Island to the south. Currents can be strong in that area. The water's deep, and storms make the situation even worse, which is what happened."

"Keith Allen was supposed to pick the kids up?"

Palmer nodded. "But he had driven to Atlanta and didn't return until later that night."

"So the teens were stranded."

"And in the water when the storm hit. After all the booze they'd consumed, getting to shore became a problem. Hayden and Cindy jumped from the rope swing. She hurt her arm. Supposedly Hayden hit the water hard. He may have been knocked unconscious or got caught in the current."

"And was never seen again?"

"Until the underwater crew pulled his body to the surface."

"How'd Stephanie Upton get involved?"

"Ted had called her earlier, when Keith didn't show, and said they needed a ride back to the mainland. By the time she arrived, the storm was in full fury, and the kids were struggling in the water. To her credit, Stephanie rescued everyone except Hayden."

Brody's heart ached for her. No wonder Stephanie didn't want to face her aunt or didn't have a more forthright relationship with her surviving cousin.

"Did you talk to Keith after the incident?"

"He was pretty shaken. Blamed himself for being held up in Atlanta."

"What about Mrs. Allen?"

Palmer shook his head. "She was never the same after her son's death. It was as if the life had been taken from her, as well. Not long thereafter, she had a stroke. Probably the stress and grief."

"Hayden had a red Ford pickup truck, mud tires. Supposedly, it was sold at auction. You know anything about it?"

"Easy enough to find out. Earl Lear runs the only auction in this area. I'll call him." The chief reached for his phone and tapped in a series of digits.

He rubbed his chin. "Hey, Earl, this is Chief Palmer. I need some information about that red, jacked-up truck Hayden Allen used to drive." He nodded. "Can you tell me who bought it?"

Palmer eyed Brody and pulled his mouth away from the receiver. "Earl's checking his records. Shouldn't be too hard to track down the buyer."

Palmer reached for a pen and positioned a small tablet on his desk. "I'm ready to copy."

He jotted a name and phone number on the paper. "Thanks, Earl."

The cop rewrote the message, tore the page from the spiral notebook and handed it to Brody. "The truck sold to a Sam Franken. The guy lives on a rural route not far from Montgomery over in Alabama. You think it might be the same truck that Stephanie Upton mentioned yesterday?"

"I have no idea, but both vehicles fit the same relative description."

"We'll pull Department of Motor Vehicle records and check on any trucks, red in color, belonging to folks in this area. Could be a lengthy list, but I'll let you know what we find."

"Sounds good, Chief." Brody gave his card to Palmer and then dropped the disposable cup in the trash. "Appreciate the coffee and your time. I'll be in touch."

Brody left the station with more information than he had expected. Just as he had feared, Ted had been on a downward spiral in high school. The military may have helped to straighten him out, but he still had a problem when it came to his sister. A bigger problem than anyone, except Brody, seemed to realize.

EIGHT

After glancing at her watch for the fourth time, Stephanie pushed away from her desk and shoved the papers she was working on into her bottom drawer. Grabbing her purse and tote, she changed clothes and shoes in the restroom and left the office to wait for Brody outside. As a rule, military guys were punctual, and his car turned into the lot before she reached the sidewalk.

"I hate pulling you away from your CID work, Brody." He bounded around the front of the car and stood holding the passenger door for her, which made her smile. He, too, had changed and was dressed in a polo and khaki slacks and Top-Siders. His phone was strapped to his waist. Knowing how conscientious Brody was, he'd probably used an ankle holster for his service weapon.

His smile was warm and welcoming as he climbed behind the wheel. "I stopped by city hall. The clerk said Keith reserved the entire picnic area some months ago, and since then, Freemont Real Estate matched the municipal funds so the facilities would be ready to use."

"Did you find out what's available?"

"There's a large kitchen, an outdoor dining pavilion and restrooms. They've installed a playground for kids and have wheelchair ramps, which will be perfect for any of the military who aren't mobile. Evidently they're still working to shore up some of the trails. Signs are posted on areas under construction that need to be avoided."

"Keith emailed me a couple hours ago. His message included an itinerary for the day, including volleyball and a fun run."

"Sounds as if your cousin has turned into a staunch military supporter."

"Which makes me glad."

The sunshine coming through the window cheered Stephanie's spirits, and the change of scenery helped improve her outlook. Taking a drive on this lovely summer day was just what she needed.

She and Brody talked about everything except her brother or Josh or bedsheets painted with a bull's-eye. By the time they arrived at the marina, she was feeling refreshed, but once she glanced at her father's cabin cruiser moored to the dock, her stomach soured.

She walked to where Keith stood looking out at the lake. Brody was a step behind. He quickly caught up with her and smiled as if offering support.

Keith greeted them warmly and then said, "I expect the others should be here soon. You can wait with me or go on ahead."

Brody glanced at the boats, staring long and hard at her father's sleek cabin cruiser. The Upton Queen was painted in fancy script along the side of the sturdy craft.

"My father's pride and joy," she said, then pointed to a small motorboat tied nearby. "I prefer *The Princess*."

"Is it yours?"

"By default. Dad got the boat for my mother, but she never shared his affinity for the water."

"Stephanie takes after her father on that count," Keith volunteered. "He loves boats and anything nautical."

A Dodge Dart pulled into the lot. Nikki and Cindy climbed out from the backseat. Ted and Paul slammed the front doors and headed toward the docks with the girls close behind.

"Looks like you'll have a lot of folks to transport," Stephanie said to Keith. "Brody and I'll ride over on *The Princess*."

She waved to Ted. "Do you want to go with me?"

He shook his head. "I'll stay with Paul."

Stephanie sighed. Why had she even asked?

"Walt said we could use his boat," Cindy volunteered.

Stephanie appreciated her willingness to help. "That's not necessary. Keith has room for all of you. Brody and I will meet you on the island."

Brody helped Stephanie untie the mooring lines and then sat next to her as she maneuvered *The Princess* out of the marina. Overhead, a gull cawed.

She glanced back to where Nikki leaned against the dock and pulled at a lock of her hair over and over again. Keith stood on the deck of his craft. Cindy motioned for everyone to follow him onboard.

Brody sighed with satisfaction once they headed into open water. "It's like another world."

"I used to come here often as a kid." She increased the throttle and raised her voice over the motor. "When I got older I did competitive swimming and spent most of my time training at an indoor pool with my team. Life got busy, and I forgot how much I loved the lake." She turned and smiled at him. "Growing up in L.A., you must have spent time at the beach."

He shook his head. "My mom never took me. I learned to swim at summer camp."

"Summer camp? Sounds like you were a privileged kid," she teased.

"Hardly. Dad left when I was twelve and my mother worked two jobs to make ends meet. Luckily, a church in the suburbs ran a two-week camp for needy kids."

"Any siblings?"

He shook his head. "Spoiled only child."

If money was tight, Stephanie doubted Brody had anything extra growing up. In contrast, she had taken so many things for granted in her youth, yet what she wanted most had always eluded her.

"Do you miss your dad?" she asked.

"At times. Although even when he was there he wasn't interested in being a parent."

Stephanie could relate. "My mother always called my father a good provider."

"Meaning he worked long hours and was never home?"

She nodded. "That was pretty much the case. Mom tried to make it up to us. Ted didn't seem to mind, but I remembered when I was younger and Dad was around more." She laughed ruefully. "You know kids. They blame themselves. I always thought if I worked harder, he'd be proud of me, and life would return to the way it had been."

"So you swam on teams and loved the water to get his attention."

"Silly, huh?"

"Not at all. I joined the military to become what my father wasn't."

"What made you decide to go into the CID?"

His gaze narrowed. "A friend of mine died in a violent crime on post. I wanted to right that wrong."

Stephanie heard the pain in his voice. "I'm sorry, Brody." She expected him to share more about what had happened, but he stared at the water and remained silent.

Once *The Princess* was secured at the small dock on the island, they headed to the picnic area. Keith and the others soon joined them there.

Ted and Nikki had paired up. Paul stood next to Cindy and listened while Keith gave an overview of the itinerary.

"Nikki, you're supervising the kitchen. Some local folks will be helping. Make sure the place is clean and tidy by the time we pack up and head back to the marina. Probably about five o'clock."

He turned to Cindy. "You volunteered for the zip line and adventure climb. A couple of the sergeants from the WTB will help you."

She nodded. "I'll be happy for their help."

"If the weather cooperates, swimming will be an option. The city's providing paddleboats and a pontoon."

Stephanie raised her hand to get Keith's attention. "I'll need to get medical approval for some of the soldiers to take part in the more strenuous activities."

"That works for me." Keith glanced at his watch. "Check out the area and let's meet back here in about half an hour."

Brody followed Cindy up the hill to inspect the zip line while Stephanie headed into the kitchen. She was impressed by the cleanliness of the entire facility, including the latrines and first-aid station.

Once back at the meeting area, she gazed upward at the tall tower and the steel-cord zip line that ran across the narrow channel, from Big Island to neighboring Small Island.

Concerned about the dangerous currents that swept between the two bodies of land, Stephanie turned to Keith. "Can you call the city to be sure the zip line meets all safety regulations?"

"I've already done that. It's up to code." He pointed to a narrow path visible in the distance. "There's even a rope footbridge the soldiers can walk over that connects the islands. Supposedly there's a park on the other side. We've got time if you want to check it out."

"It shouldn't take me long."

Inhaling the sweet smell of the honeysuckle, Stephanie made her way along the path that led to the rocky gorge separating the two islands. Looking down, she saw the churning current that crashed against the cement slabs brought in to shore up the sides of the island from erosion.

Up close, the hanging bridge didn't appear as sturdy as she would have hoped. Two ropes anchored the wooden decking into metal eyehooks embedded in cement. Additional ropes served as handrails and protective side webbing. Glancing across to the opposite island, she saw a garden of wildflowers and a number of park benches. Surely the bridge was more than adequate for foot traffic.

Grabbing hold of the thick hemp railings, she stepped onto the wooden deck. The platform swayed. She looked down. Tiny eddies swirled below as the water surged through the narrow passageway.

Her weight shifted ever so slightly. She took a step forward and then another, trying to steady herself.

The sound of footsteps on the path caused her to turn.

Too quickly.

The bridge responded to the movement, throwing her off balance. She grabbed the rope railing and tugged on the hemp to steady herself.

Out of the corner of her eye, she spotted a rush of motion. Someone lunged from the underbrush and hunkered down on the path as if to tie his shoe.

In a flash, he was gone.

She took another step forward.

Crack.

One of the supporting anchors gave way. The deck collapsed underfoot, leaving her dangling above the water. With her heart lodged in her throat, she frantically clawed to get a toehold. White-knuckled, her fingers clutched the railing. The thick hemp cut into her flesh.

"Help!"

She screamed again and again, but the effort went unnoticed. A wave of vertigo swept over her. She clenched her jaw, refusing to give in to the roll of nausea or the fear that had turned her blood to ice. If she let go of the rope, she'd fall into the raging waters below.

High above her, she saw the zip line platform. Brody and Cindy were probably at the park, waiting for her to meet them there. They didn't realize she was in trouble.

Deadly trouble.

"Where's Stephanie?" Brody asked when he rejoined Keith at the picnic area.

"The last I saw of her, she was heading to the footbridge." Keith glanced at the sky. "Dark clouds are rolling in. We'd better start back to the mainland."

"Don't leave until I find Stephanie," Brody said as he hurried along the path.

Worried, he called her name. His eyes flicked right and then left, hoping to catch sight of her.

Rounding a curve in the path, he saw the broken bridge in the distance and screamed to the others for help as he raced forward. His stomach lurched with fear, seeing her dangling above the water.

"B-Brody?"

"I'm right here." Quickly, he realized the danger of

adding more weight to the already-compromised suspension bridge. "I need you to inch toward me. One hand at a time."

"I…I can't."

"Yes, you can." Holding on to a nearby sapling for support, he reached forward, stretching his hand to meet hers. "Take it slow."

"My arms—"

"I'll have you in a minute. Work your way to me."

Ever so slowly, she moved her fingers along the rope, until—in one swift motion—he grabbed her and pulled her to safety.

She collapsed into his embrace, trembling. "Oh, Brody."

"It's okay. You're safe now."

"I…I heard someone on the path. He came from nowhere. All I saw was a gray sweatshirt. The hood covered his head. He…he knelt down for a moment. I thought he was tying his shoe."

Brody examined the rope that supported the wooden deck. Somehow, it had frayed loose from the anchoring rod. "Did you recognize the guy?"

She shook her head.

"Was it Ted?"

She pulled back. "No."

"But it was a man?" Brody asked.

"That's right. He was wearing a gray sweatshirt."

"Like the army PT uniform?"

She threw up her hands and shrugged as if annoyed with his questions. "I don't know whether it was military. I didn't see a logo."

Letting out a frustrated sigh, Brody glanced at the darkening sky. "Let's head to the boat. It looks like we're in for rain."

Before they returned to the path, he looked down at the gorge, thinking of what could have been. His gut tightened when he spotted something shiny wedged in the rocks below. A metal sign attached to a chain.

Danger. Do Not Cross. Bridge Closed for Repair.

The sign at some point had hung across the entrance to the bridge, warning pedestrians. Had it blown free in the wind? Or had someone removed the sign and then tampered with the already-frayed support rope?

What about the man in the gray sweatshirt? Did he stop to tie his shoe or was he doing something else—something to cause the bridge to collapse?

NINE

Stephanie leaned against Brody as they hurried along the path. Her legs were weak and her arms felt like jelly. The palms of her hands were scraped and raw, but those were minor problems considering what the outcome would have been if Brody hadn't found her.

Approaching the picnic area, he ushered her to a bench. "Can I get you some water?"

She shook her head. "I'm okay."

"What happened?" Keith asked as he neared.

Brody explained about the collapsed bridge and Stephanie's near catastrophe. "Who told her about the footbridge?"

"I did." Keith pointed to himself. "But I didn't know there was a problem."

"Have you seen anyone else, except our group, on the island?"

"No, but I've been in this area the entire time."

"What's going on?" Cindy asked as she and Nikki hurried toward them.

"Did either of you notice any other visitors on the island?"

Nikki shook her head. "I thought we were the only ones here."

Cindy pointed to the zip line. "I saw a jon boat leaving the small dock on the far side of the island when I was on the tower."

"What color?" Brody asked.

She blew out a breath and shook her head. "Ah, dark. Maybe navy. Maybe black. No name on the hull. Outboard motor. One guy, but I can't tell you what he looked like at that distance."

"What was he wearing?"

Cindy shrugged. "Hard to tell. A beige shirt. Or maybe it was gray."

"Heavy? Thin? Old? Young?"

She threw up her hands. "It was too far to tell. Plus, I didn't realize he was important. Just a guy out fishing."

Brody called the Freemont police and had them contact the manager of the marina in case he saw anyone in a jon boat heading back from Big Island. He also requested law enforcement search the island as soon as possible and keep their eyes open for a man in a gray sweatshirt.

Disconnecting, he glanced around. "Where are Paul and Ted?"

"Probably still on the ridge," Keith said. "They were checking the trail for the fun run."

"Were they hanging around the footbridge?" Brody glanced at Cindy.

She shook her head. "Not that I saw."

Brody nodded and then eyed the sky. "We need to

head back to the marina soon. I'll check the ridge." He double-timed up the trail.

Cindy noticed Stephanie's scraped hands. "I saw some antiseptic ointment in the first-aid station."

"Thanks, but I'm okay. Just give me a minute to get my heartbeat back to normal."

"Oh, Stephanie." Nikki gave her a quick hug. "I'm so glad you're okay."

The three women talked for a few minutes until Stephanie glanced over her shoulder and saw Paul and Ted some distance away, standing in front of a three-foot stone monument she hadn't noticed earlier. Ted doubled over and dropped his head into his hands.

She turned to Keith. "Go after Brody. Tell him the guys are back."

"Will do."

Stephanie hurried to join her brother and Paul, but stopped short when she neared the monument. Her heart lodged in her throat.

Hayden Allen City Park.

A lovely tribute that had upset Ted.

She caught up to her brother at the dock and grabbed his sleeve. He jerked out of her hold.

"It's been three years, Ted. You've got to let go of the painful memories."

He pointed an accusatory finger back at her. "What about you? How have you dealt with the past?"

"Not very well," she admitted with a low voice.

"Then don't tell me how I should behave." He turned and stared at Paul, then Nikki, who had moved closer.

"Hayden was the best of us. Only he's gone, and we have to pretend that it's okay, but it's not."

He flicked his gaze back to Stephanie. "Life isn't fair, which is what you used to tell me when Mom was sick. I didn't want to listen to anything you had to say back then. I don't want your advice now, either."

"Ted, please."

"Don't worry. I'll attend the picnic and help the guys and gals who are worse off than I am. After all, I'm not hurt on the outside. My only scars are from the burns on my legs and those have healed, but there are bigger scars on the inside, and they're still festering. Or maybe you haven't noticed."

"I want to help you."

"Then stay out of my life. You've done enough to remind me of the past. Don't butt in where you're not wanted."

Ted stomped aboard Keith's boat.

Stephanie turned to see Brody standing near the monument. A frown covered his square face. If he had been waiting for some sign of dysfunction from her brother, surely he had heard enough today to fill a computer file. Ted kept digging a bigger hole for himself.

Brody followed the guys onto Keith's boat and talked to each of them privately. No doubt he was trying to determine if they'd removed the sign from the bridge or tampered with one of the supporting ropes. He also searched the boat and the girls' handbags.

"Your brother will come around, Steph," Keith said as he approached and patted her shoulder.

She sighed. "Did you ever wonder why everything turned out the way it did, Keith? Is it something about our families that causes so much pain?"

He shook his head. "My mom said it was inevitable when Hayden drowned. I never understood what she meant. I often thought there was something she didn't want me to know."

"Like what?"

"I'm not sure. Hayden and I were so different, as if we weren't even brothers. My parents used to argue. Mom always took Hayden's side. After he died, I could never compete with his memory. That's a tough place to be, the underdog. You never had to deal with that. You were the favored child."

"Only because I worked to earn my father's approval." She turned and looked back over the water. "What I really wanted was his love."

Once they were back onboard *The Princess*, Brody applied ointment to Stephanie's hands and wrapped them in gauze. He watched the darkening sky while she navigated the craft into deep water.

Neither of them spoke about Stephanie's close call or whether the guy in the gray sweatshirt had done something to cause the bridge to collapse. Ted had always been a logical suspect in Brody's mind, but this time Keith had encouraged her to explore the park on the smaller island, an excursion that could have claimed her life.

In addition, Ted and Paul's stories had matched when Brody questioned them. They had explored the route for the fun run and never ventured near the footbridge.

The entire island had been visible from the ridge. Brody hadn't seen anyone else on the island, and the jon boat had long disappeared from view.

When he got back to post, he would contact the police in case the marina manager had identified the boat owner. Another long shot; there seemed to be too many, especially when it came to Stephanie's well-being.

So far, she'd escaped injury, other than her scraped palms, but if Brody hadn't found her today—

He couldn't think about what ifs. He had to think about what he knew to be fact. Right now, he had no evidence and lots of suspicions.

Stephanie was visibly relieved when they reached the marina. So was Brody. He wanted to get her back to post safe and sound. Keith had already docked. Ted and Paul were in the parking lot.

"Come on." Nikki motioned to Cindy, who stood at the end of the pier. The wind whipped at her blouse. Her hair flew around her face. She pushed it back with one hand and clutched the railing with the other.

Brody hopped onto the dock and approached the distraught woman. "Cindy, you need to get in the car before it starts to rain."

She turned, tears in her eyes. "I…I didn't think it would affect me like this. I try to be strong, but coming back made everything worse."

Keith took her arm. "It's okay, Cindy. I'll drive you

home." He helped her into his car and followed Paul and the others out of the parking lot.

"I wonder if this was the first time Cindy has been at the lake since Hayden's death?" Brody said, once he and Stephanie were inside his car, just as the rain started to fall.

"You go through a tragedy like that and you never want to go back to where it happened."

"Should you cancel the picnic?" he asked.

"That would only hurt the soldiers who are looking forward to the day. I'll encourage Ted to stay at the barracks. Maybe he and Paul can do something together."

"He never should have come today."

She nodded. "Keith probably invited him. Or maybe Paul insisted he come."

"How are your hands?"

"Better. Thanks for taking care of them."

He turned the windshield wipers to high and pulled onto the road to Fort Rickman.

"What was Keith doing in Atlanta the day his brother died?"

She hesitated before saying, "I think he used Atlanta as an excuse. He and his friends often partied at a campsite north of town. Alcohol was usually involved."

"Did he know about Hayden's drinking?"

"I'm sure he did."

"Because?"

She stared out the window and failed to answer.

"Stephanie—"

She shrugged and glanced back at him, her expression pained. "Keith took the boys to the island that day and said he would pick them up by three o'clock."

"Not much time to drive to Atlanta and back. Is that why you think he was in the local area?"

"That's my opinion only."

"How did the boys get the alcohol?"

"Supposedly they found the bottles on the island. They all told the same story. Folks were upset about Hayden's death. No one gave much thought to the alcohol with a dead teen to mourn." She shook her head. "Especially since it was Hayden."

"I'm sure the townspeople would have been upset no matter who had died."

"It's just—" She sighed. "It was as if the whole town was counting on Hayden to succeed. Everyone expected so much from him."

"What about Paul? How did he play into the group?"

"His parents have a house in the Country Club subdivision, not far from ours, so he and Ted were friends growing up."

"Didn't Hayden and Keith live in the Estates, as well?"

"That's right. Josh was the only one who wasn't close by. All the boys were in the same grade, but Hayden was six months younger. He started hanging out with the guys his senior year."

Brody reached for her hand and gently wove his fingers through hers, taking care not to hurt her scraped skin. "I read the newspaper archives of the rescue. You were able to save the other kids. That's got to give you some sense of satisfaction."

"The papers didn't print the whole story."

"So you tell me what happened."

"I was exhausted and couldn't dive deep enough or stay down long enough to save Hayden. That's what no one talks about."

"The article said you had to be pulled from the water."

"I…I wanted to keep searching," she admitted. "I tried to save him. I just don't know if I tried hard enough."

"Stephanie, you gave it your all."

"You weren't there, Brody."

"No, but I know how determined you are to take care of your brother. You don't give up."

She glanced down at their hands, then pulled hers away and looked out the window.

Brody knew about looking back. Nothing good came from replaying what couldn't be changed. When he met Stephanie, something had sparked to life within him, a part he thought had died long ago.

If he determined Ted was to blame for Joshua's injury, there would be no hope for a relationship with Stephanie. The situation would be even more impossible if Ted had marked her bedding or damaged the bridge today. Although he doubted Stephanie realized that he wanted to help Ted, his first priority was to keep her safe.

After arriving on post, Stephanie and Brody stopped at the hospital to check on Joshua. They rode the elevator to the third floor and walked together into the ICU.

"We're here to see Private Joshua Webb." Brody showed his CID identification to the clerk on duty.

"He won't be able to answer questions at this time."

"I understand. But I still need to see him."

The clerk pointed down the hallway. "Room six. On the left."

Stephanie inhaled a quick breath as she neared Joshua's bedside. His eyes were closed and his face was ashen. He was hooked up to a number of machines that pumped meds and took vital signs at regular intervals.

Brody touched his shoulder. "It's CID Special Agent Goodman. Can you hear me, Joshua?"

He nodded ever so slightly.

"Do you remember who did this to you?"

Stephanie glanced at the heart monitor. Josh's rate increased slightly. "This isn't a good time, Brody."

"I need information, Stephanie. The investigation is stagnant. If Josh can identify who attacked him, we'll be able to put that person behind bars before someone else is hurt."

"The nurse said no questions," she insisted.

"Actually, she said he wouldn't be able to answer questions, but he can blink." Brody glanced back at the patient. "I know you can hear me, Josh. If you saw the person who attacked you, blink twice. If you didn't see anyone, blink once."

The response was immediate. Joshua blinked twice.

"Was it someone you knew?" Brody pressed.

Once again, Josh blinked twice.

"I'm going to mention a few people. Blink if I say the name of the person who attacked you."

Stephanie didn't like the direction of the questioning. "Brody, you're pushing him too hard. If he's medicated, the blinking could be an involuntary response."

Brody glanced at her. "What are you worried about, Stephanie?"

She couldn't give voice to her concern that Brody's bedside interrogation could lead to incorrect information. Information that might incriminate Ted.

"Was it Paul Massey?" Brody asked.

Joshua's eyes remained closed.

"Brody, please."

"Listen carefully, Joshua. Was it—"

A noise sounded behind them.

Stephanie turned to see her brother, standing in the doorway, red faced and angered. Paul stood next to him.

"You shouldn't be here, Ted. You were upset at the marina. Don't upset yourself more."

Ted pushed past her to the bed and grabbed Josh's hand. "Hey, buddy, you hold on. Keep fighting. This is just another battle like we saw in Afghanistan. You can do it."

A nurse in scrubs entered the room. "All of you need to leave."

"Joshua, was it—" Brody pressed.

"Sir, please." The nurse's voice was firm.

"Come on, Ted." Stephanie took her brother's arm. He jerked out of her hold and left the room, with Paul trailing close behind.

Stephanie glanced back at Brody, who followed her

into the hallway. As much as he thought he was trying to help, Brody was making everything worse, for Joshua, for Ted and even for herself.

TEN

Frustrated to learn the new tires hadn't yet arrived, Stephanie accepted a ride from Brody to work the following morning.

"I hate to put you out," she said when he picked her up. His starched white shirt and paisley tie complemented his ruddy skin and brought out the flecks of gold in his eyes. As he held the door for her, she realized his gentlemanly manners and thoughtfulness were having an effect on her in a good way.

How easily she took to the little things he did that showed the respect he had for women. Her own father hadn't been one to fawn over her mother, and growing up, many of the boys in town took a more chauvinistic outlook toward the fairer sex. Stephanie had to admit she enjoyed the pampered way Brody made her feel.

"Major Jenkins said you're coming to the Warrior Transitional Battalion this afternoon to talk to some of the soldiers."

Brody nodded. "We were firming up the details the day you called the WTB. Keeping the groups small is best, so we worked out a schedule that allows me to talk to each company individually."

"That's perfect. They'll feel more comfortable in a smaller environment. Major Jenkins said you wanted to start with Ted's company."

"I thought the session might pull down some of the barriers he's put up," Brody said. "You saw how he broke down at the marina. Plus, I want the other soldiers in his unit to be aware of the signs of PTSD and know the CID is a source of help if they feel in danger or threatened in any way."

"Just don't single Ted out from the bunch."

Brody's brow furrowed. "You think I'd do that?"

She noticed a hint of disappointment in his voice. "I'm not saying you'd do anything wrong, Brody, but I want this to be a healing situation for my brother, not one that would do more harm."

"I've given this class a number of times on other posts, Stephanie. You can trust me to be sensitive to everyone's needs."

She pulled in a deep breath and turned her gaze to the overcast sky. Brody was a strong man who stood for truth and justice. That stance could seem intimidating to some, including her brother, who had always struggled with his own self-worth.

Just so Brody, with his prying questions, didn't seem like a threat. More than anything, she wanted him to reach out to Ted.

Brody could be such a good role model for her brother and someone Ted could look up to and try to emulate. He could use a mentor, especially since their own dad had never been a positive influence in her brother's life.

As much as she wanted Ted and Brody to connect, she feared the session later today would give Ted more fuel to light the fire of indignation that seemed to consume him these days.

Her brother was walking a fine line between health and breakdown. His buddy Josh's injury only compounded the situation.

Stephanie would attend the class to ensure the information Brody presented to the company didn't hamper Ted's progress, although she wasn't sure getting between her brother and the CID agent would be a positive experience, either for Ted or for herself.

Brody arrived at the Warrior Transitional Battalion ahead of schedule. He had hoped to see Stephanie and spend time with her before the soldiers arrived, but she was nowhere to be found. Trying to mask his disappointment, he arranged the chairs in the conference room and checked the thermostat on the air conditioner. He wanted the soldiers to be comfortable and receptive to the information he would provide.

Once the room was ready, the soldiers filtered in and claimed their chairs. A number of them had suffered significant injuries, including loss of limbs and scars that were hard to ignore. Brody was humbled by the sacrifice of so many who put country before self.

Some of the military personnel, both male and female, had less noticeable injuries. Theirs were the hidden wounds of trauma and the stress of living in a war zone.

Ted shuffled into the room and took a seat close to the door. Brody nodded in his direction, but the PFC averted his gaze and toyed with his smart phone.

Brody checked his watch, hoping Stephanie would be able to attend the program. A hint of concern made the hairs on his neck raise. He tried to shake off his worry and focus instead on the men and women gathered for the talk.

Major Jenkins approached, holding out his hand, which Brody accepted. "Thanks again for being with us today."

"My pleasure, sir." Brody looked around the room. "Do you have any idea where Stephanie Upton might be?"

"She was in her office earlier. I'm sure she'll show up soon."

"I'll leave a seat for her." Brody positioned a chair close to the door. Hearing the clip of heels, he peered into the hallway and saw her racing toward the classroom. A sense of relief swept over him.

"Sorry." A sincere smile tugged at her lips as she hurried into the room. "I was talking to the medical case manager about one of my soldiers."

"No problem. You're here in plenty of time." Brody was taken by the way her hair danced on her shoulders. The sun coming through the window accentuated the golden highlights.

The room quieted as the major walked to the microphone. He quickly provided background information about Brody, including his tours in combat and the list of his medals and awards. "We're fortunate to have him with us today and welcome the information he will provide."

"Thank you, Major Jenkins." Using a PowerPoint program, Brody worked through a series of slides that provided statistics about the prevalence of PTSD, as well as warning signs and interventions.

"In addition to the symptoms we've talked about, any traumatic injury or experience, whether war related or not, can also lead to memory problems, such as short-term amnesia."

He pointed around the room. "Any of you could fall victim to this disease because of your time in combat. Whether you were injured because of an IED, bullets or mortars, you've been wounded physically, but you've had a psychological trauma, too. Be alert to changes in temperament and behavior. If you know the warning signs and watch out for one another, a more serious situation could be stopped before it gets out of hand."

Stephanie's gaze was warm and encouraging, and the men and women in uniform seemed interested. Many of them leaned forward in their chairs and all of them listened attentively to what Brody was sharing.

"Remember, PTSD can affect anyone, whether military or civilian. Any trauma can cause PTSD and often the symptoms don't appear until well after the event occurred. If you have PTSD, you're not alone. More than fifty percent of our wounded warriors experience PTSD in one form or another. So don't keep any struggle bottled up inside you. Your medical-care team is ready to help. Counselors are always available, and the CID is eager to support you, as well."

When he finished the talk, he opened the floor for questions.

One of the men raised his hand. "What about someone who can't sleep and wanders the barracks at night?"

"I'd say the advocate or medical-care team should be made aware of the situation so the soldier can receive the help he or she needs."

The guy who had posed the question turned to look at Ted, who squirmed in his seat.

"Talk to him, Ted," another soldier prompted. "Tell the special agent about the dreams you've been having."

Ted's eyes narrowed. "Hey, guys, what are you talking about?"

"You don't have to hide it," one of the men called out.

Ted glanced at Brody and then turned to look at Stephanie.

She started to stand. "Maybe we should—"

"Did you plan to gang up on me?" Ted demanded.

"Of course not." Stephanie approached her brother.

He stood and pointed his finger at Brody. "You set me up for this."

Brody moved forward. "I came here to talk about PTSD, Ted. If you've got some of the symptoms, you need help."

"Help?" He flicked his gaze between Stephanie

and Brody. "I don't appreciate being the center of a witch hunt."

"That's not what this is," Stephanie objected.

"Isn't it?" He pushed past her and rushed from the room.

She turned and stared at Brody for a brief moment as if he were to blame.

He wanted to reach for her and hold her until the accusation that flashed from her eyes calmed into acceptance. Hard though it was for Stephanie to realize, she wasn't at fault and neither was he.

Ted was struggling with issues that were too difficult for him to handle alone. His reactions today, yesterday and the day before proved how fragile he was at this time.

Stephanie's face clouded. She blinked rapidly and then turned and hurried out of the room.

Brody had wanted to see what type of a reaction Ted would have to the information about PTSD, but he hadn't expected everything to explode. Nor had he thought that Ted would strike out so forcefully at Stephanie.

The last thing Brody wanted was to cause her more pain. She'd had enough already.

As he watched her flee the room, memories from Brody's past surfaced again. So painful, so raw, even after all these years. He remembered his own struggle and the counselor who had been his rock when all he could see was darkness.

Brody knew too well about PTSD and the insidious hold it had on its victims. Just like a flesh-and-blood enemy, the disease had to be combated aggressively. If only Ted would realize he needed help.

The soldiers continued to field questions, and the session concluded on a high note, for which Brody was glad. Had Ted stayed, he might have realized that the WTB, the cadre and medical-care team—and even the other soldiers—were working together for the betterment of all.

Once the military personnel had gone back to their unit, Brody gathered his notes and hurried from the classroom, determined to find Stephanie. He wanted to talk to her about Ted's condition and what he could do to offer support and encouragement.

But recalling the way Stephanie had looked at him, Brody feared she wouldn't want to see him now. He wasn't sure she would ever want to see him again.

Stephanie ran after Ted, but he had disappeared by the time she got outside. Hearing the rev of an engine, she turned and saw Paul's blue Dodge Dart leaving the WTB parking area.

Letting out a long sigh, she raked her hand through her hair. At least Ted wasn't alone. Hopefully, Paul would be a listening ear, which Ted needed.

If only he would open up and share his pain, not only the pain from the IED explosion and war injuries, but also the pain from their mother's death and the tragedy that had claimed Hayden's life. The combined toll on Ted was all too evident today.

She made a mental note to notify his counselor and the other members of his care team about the hard time her brother was having. Shaking her head, she almost laughed at the understatement. Ted's condition was far worse than she had previously thought. Why had she refused to see the truth? Perhaps because she always felt responsible for her younger brother.

The other soldiers in his unit were aware of the situation. She should have been, as well.

Shame on her.

If she had ignored the signals from Ted, no telling what she had missed from the other men.

Discouraged and wondering if she could ever be effective in her job, Stephanie headed back to her office.

Brody was waiting for her.

The warmth she saw in his gaze told her more than words. He didn't blame her for her brother's outburst. Nor did Brody think she had let Ted down, which was what she wanted to believe but couldn't.

Ever since their mother had died, Stephanie had tried to fill the gaps in Ted's life. If he failed, she considered herself at fault. Everything changed that day on the lake when she'd finally realized her brother had to take responsibility for his own actions.

Tough love, some called it. At the time, she thought she was making the best decision for Ted.

Yet nothing good had come from it. Only more pain.

Hayden had died, and she would carry the guilt of that burden for the rest of her life.

"Ted didn't mean what he said, Stephanie." Brody stepped closer, his voice filled with concern.

She tried to smile. "He's so confused right now and

struggling with so many issues. I thought I could help him, but I can't seem to do anything right."

"You love him, and that's what he needs most."

Brody rubbed his hand over her shoulder, his touch soothing away her frustration.

"All I want is for Ted to heal," she finally whispered.

"Let me help you."

Stephanie had been alone for so long. She needed someone to lean on, at least for a while. Someone who cared about her and accepted her, despite her failings.

Brody opened his arms and she stepped into his embrace. Feeling secure at long last, she rested her head on his chest and took comfort in hearing the steady beat of his heart. Her own struggle eased as if being in Brody's arms had the power to transform the pain she carried into something whole and healed.

"I'm so sorry," he said, his voice husky with emotion.

His breath warmed her cheek. She nestled closer, knowing the moment would pass too soon and she'd return to being an advocate for soldiers who had faced horrific traumas. She needed to be strong in order to help them. She needed to be even stronger to help Ted.

Right now, she was grateful for Brody, who wanted to help her, and more than anything, she wanted to remain wrapped in his arms.

After Brody left her office, Stephanie received a phone call from Ted's counselor. Her brother had kept his appointment and seemed eager for the next session. Although he didn't share specifically what had been discussed, the counselor was enthusiastic about the progress that had been made.

Ted was taking positive steps forward. With medication for his anxiety and depression, and additional counseling sessions, the counselor felt fairly confident that Ted could turn everything around.

Stephanie's spirits soared with the news, but her optimism plummeted when Major Jenkins called soon thereafter and shared that Ted had asked to be taken off her caseload.

"I won't act on his request at this point," the major said. "See what you can do to change Ted's mind. Besides, I know you have your brother's best interest at heart."

She hung up feeling conflicted. How could she reach her brother when he remained closed to any attempt on her part to help?

After what had happened today, she wasn't sure their relationship would ever improve. No matter what she did, the divide between them just kept getting bigger.

ELEVEN

Brody checked with the WTB first sergeant to ensure Ted headed back to the barracks after his counseling appointment. The sergeant promised to keep him busy around the battalion. He also promised to call Brody if Ted showed any signs of depression or aggravation.

Once he returned to his office, Brody kept thinking of Stephanie and realized his distraction would continue until he called her.

Hearing her voice when she answered made him smile and ask if she wanted to join him for dinner that evening.

"There's a restaurant in Alabama about an hour's drive from Freemont that has an outdoor patio and lots of atmosphere. Plus, the cooking is the best in the area that I've found."

"The Tadwell Inn?" she asked.

"You know the place."

"And love going there. But I have a meeting this afternoon that will probably run until five or five-thirty."

"Five-thirty works for me," Brody said. "I've got a number of loose ends to tie up around here."

His next phone call was to the farmer in Alabama. The man that answered sounded like a no-nonsense, salt-of-the-earth type of guy.

Brody identified himself and then said, "Sir, I'm calling about the Ford truck you bought three years ago at an auction in Freemont, Georgia."

"The Ford's long gone, Agent Goodman."

"How's that?"

"Totaled."

"Did you have the truck repaired?"

"What don't you understand about totaled? The Lord saved me, but He destroyed the Ford." The farmer sighed. "Only good thing was that I was driving instead of my son. I ended up with a few cuts and bruises. Nothing serious. Doubt my boy would have been as lucky. He's got a lead foot like his late mother."

"I'm sorry about your wife, sir."

"Appreciate the condolences. Sandra was a fine woman. The Lord took her too early."

Brody empathized with the man's loss.

"I had to accept the Lord's will for my life, in spite of my grief and loneliness," Mr. Franken continued, seeming eager to talk.

"Yes, sir."

"He's given me a fine son, even though he has a heavy foot on the gas pedal." The farmer chuckled. "Plus a daughter-in-law and a grandbaby on the way. I miss my wife, but I've got folks to love. God made me look to the future, which helped me overcome my grief."

"I'm glad things are better, sir."

"Made me realize when tough times come, I need to lean on the Lord."

Brody had been told the same thing after Lisa's death. Although he didn't believe in coincidences, the repeated message seemed exactly that. Or was the Almighty sending a reminder Brody had ignored years earlier?

"Thank you, sir, for the information about the Ford. Best wishes to the new parents."

He scratched Sam Franken's name off his to-do list and called Don Palmer at the Freemont Police Department. "Hayden Allen's truck was a dead end." Brody explained about the vehicle having been totaled. "Did you get those DMV records on red pickups in the Freemont area?"

"We're checking for any of them that might have off-road tires. Nothing to report yet."

"What about the bedding and note from the Upton home?"

"The bull's-eye and X were made with a standard washable marker sold at every store that carries school or business supplies. No prints. No identifiable markings. No evidence."

"And the island search?"

"Again, nothing turned up. The city claims the danger sign blocked access to the footbridge. They have no idea who would have removed it. The rope supporting the wooden deck appeared frayed, but the integrity of the structure could have also been compromised by some external force, for whatever that's worth. No one at the marina could provide information about a fisherman in a jon boat. We're batting zero, the way I see it."

"Something will turn up," Brody said before he disconnected, although he felt anything but encouraged.

For the rest of the afternoon, he busied himself at work, but eyed the clock and counted down the minutes until he could pick up Stephanie. Once they were together, he was thankful to see some of the worry she had worn earlier had eased. Knowing Ted had gone to counseling and was now occupied at the battalion had to be a relief.

The evening drive bolstered both their spirits. Brody took a back road that wound by the river and eventually crossed into Alabama at a scenic spot that led to the heart of a small town with a picturesque square.

He turned to glance at her. A warm swirl of attraction bubbled up within him. She titled her head as if questioning why he was focused on her.

He smiled and, at that moment, the world suddenly looked brighter.

"Mind if I turn on some music?" Brody asked. "Are you a country gal?"

She laughed. "Sure. It's appropriate for the surroundings."

He selected a CD. "How about *The Best of Nashville?*"

"Perfect."

The mellow mix of guitars and banjos played softly in the background as a popular country-and-western voice opened his heart to the woman he had never expected to love.

Stephanie tapped her left hand against the console in time with the music. Brody couldn't help but notice her long, slender fingers.

Without thinking, he wrapped his hand over hers, taking care to not touch the place where the rope had rubbed her palm. He enjoyed the softness of her skin and the warmth of her hold.

She turned to smile at him, a look of genuine happiness covering her oval face. As pretty as she was, surely Stephanie had captured a number of guys' hearts. Maybe there was a special guy at her old base, Fort Stewart.

As much as Brody wanted to know, he wouldn't ask. Right now, he needed to believe he had a chance—a second chance at love.

Then he realized the truth. After everything that had happened, it was doubtful Stephanie would want anything to do with him long-term. Their paths had crossed because of the investigation. After it was over, they'd go their separate ways.

The sun had set by the time Stephanie and Brody finished dinner. She laughed as they headed back to his car. He held the door for her and touched her arm as she slipped past him onto the seat. The gesture seemed natural and filled her with a sense of peace as if some of the struggle she had felt earlier had dissipated, for which she was grateful.

During dinner, they had talked about the Wounded Warrior Program and the opportunities available to the injured. Her responsibility was to ensure the soldiers took advantage of the benefits provided for them and were able to navigate the paperwork and bureaucracy that went along with government programs.

Brody seemed genuinely concerned about the injured soldiers on her caseload, and he mentioned his own hope that Ted would be able to heal with counseling.

The trip back to Freemont passed quickly. They had turned to lighter topics, including Stephanie's high school swim team and her love of the water. Brody mentioned that he often swam laps at the indoor pool on post. Having that shared common interest made their time together even more enjoyable. Once they arrived at her house, inviting him for a swim seemed appropriate.

"I usually take a dip after dinner," she said. "Why don't you go back to your BOQ and pick up your suit?"

Brody's eyes twinkled. "Sounds great. My trunks are in my car."

Once he unlocked the door, she flipped on the entryway chandelier before disarming the security alarm. After he retrieved his gym bag, she pointed him toward a spare bedroom.

"You can change in there."

She quickly donned a one-piece suit and a cover-up and was in the kitchen when he joined her.

"Care for a cola or coffee?" she asked.

"I'll take some coffee after the swim."

She handed him a colorful beach towel. "The stairs on the deck lead down to the pool."

Brody followed her to the patio, where a wrought-iron table and chairs were positioned next to the kidney-shaped pool. Recessed lights in the landscaped area reflected across the water like tiny diamonds. A plastic raft floated in the deep end.

"I'm glad you asked me out for dinner," Stephanie said as she dropped her towel on the table.

He followed suit and placed his gym bag next to both their towels before he stepped closer. "And I'm glad you said yes."

The intensity of his gaze made her turn and point to the water. "Last one in the water makes the coffee tonight."

He grabbed her arm. "Not so fast."

She playfully tried to free herself from his hold.

His grip was strong but gentle. He pulled her closer until she was standing a breath away from him. They stopped laughing at almost the same moment. Stephanie looked into his dark eyes and saw far more than she expected.

Brody slipped his hand around her waist. She could see a pulse beating in his temple and could smell the heady scent of his aftershave. The masculine fragrance swirled around her and added to the intensity of the moment.

Gazing at his angled jaw and full lips, she felt a portion of her inner core melting, the part that worried about the past. She stared into his dark eyes and leaned closer.

"You were saying?" He smiled.

"Weren't we talking about making coffee?"

His finger twirled a strand of her hair, sending a delicious warmth pulsating along her neck.

"Are you thinking about coffee, Stephanie?" His voice was deep and dangerous.

"I'm not thinking of anything, except—"

"Except what?" His upper lip twitched ever so slightly.

Every nerve ending tingled within her.

"About whether you plan to kiss me." She closed her eyes and waited half a heartbeat until his mouth covered hers.

The night stood still. The sound of the cicadas and crickets faded into the distance. All Stephanie could focus on was the tenderness of his kiss. Gently, he drew her deeper into his embrace.

Just when she thought he would kiss her forever, Brody pulled back.

His look of need turned lighthearted. "We were heading into the water."

"We were?"

He pointed to the pool. "Last one in, remember?"

She remembered his kiss and how comfortable she had been—far too comfortable—in his arms.

Needing to reel in her emotions, she turned, took off her cover-up and dove into the pool. Before she entered the water, she heard a loud crack. Brody screamed her name.

Confused by the sharpness of his tone, she touched bottom and pushed back to the surface.

"Stay in the water." He had pulled his weapon from his gym bag and was hunkered down behind the wrought-iron table, his eyes trained on the fairway and the woods beyond. "Keep your head below the rim of the pool."

Treading water, she saw the shattered flowerpot that had sat on the table next to where they had stood only a moment ago.

He raised his cell to his ear. "This is Special Agent Goodman, Fort Rickman CID. There's been a shooting." He gave Stephanie's address. "I need police backup. Now. Notify Freemont Chief of Police Don Palmer immediately."

She followed his gaze to the dense forest. "I…I don't understand. I thought a car backfired."

"It was a gunshot, Stephanie."

Her mouth went dry. A roar filled her ears. She wanted to dive underwater and swim until her lungs burned. Surely, Brody had it all wrong.

"But—" She stared into the darkness, unable to pick out anything except the tall trees and the sounds of the night.

"Stay where you are. I'll check the area."

Bile rose in her throat. Crossing the fairway would make him an open target. In spite of the warm night, she shivered, knowing Brody could be in the line of fire.

He left the patio, but instead of heading toward the clearing, he picked his way around the neighboring houses and circled through the underbrush. She could barely make out his shadow in the darkness.

More than anything, Stephanie wanted to run inside and hide, but she knew her own safety depended on staying put. She prayed Brody would remain safe, as well.

Tears stung her eyes. She blinked them back, angry at her mixed-up emotions and inability to comprehend what was happening to her life. She and Brody had had such a nice evening, but now he was running headlong into danger.

Why hadn't he waited for backup? Because he had to be the macho cop and catch the bad guys and make sure she didn't get hurt. Much as she appreciated his protection, she couldn't take someone else getting hurt because of her. Especially not Brody.

She bit her lip, hoping to control the fear that clamped down on her chest. Listening for any sound, half expecting to hear gunfire, she counted off the minutes, not knowing who or what Brody would have to confront.

Huddled at the far edge of the pool, she inched her head up to stare into the distance, seeing nothing except the darkness.

Just when she was convinced something had happened to him, Brody stepped from the shadows. Grabbing a towel for her, he stood guard as she climbed from the pool. "Stay low and head for the back door. Someone could still be out there."

"What did you find?" she asked when they were safely inside.

"Nothing."

"Which means what?"

"Someone wanted to frighten you, or they were a

bad shot." Brody's face was tight with emotion. "Does Ted know you swim at night?"

"It's something I've always done. I…I guess so."

"He thought you'd be alone."

She shook her head and took a step back. "It wasn't Ted," she insisted.

Yet Ted and his friends had often played paintball at night with toy guns in this very same fairway in their youth.

"How can you be sure it wasn't your brother?"

"Because I know Ted."

"You know the way he was when you were growing up. He's a different person now. You've got to believe me."

The only thing she knew for sure was that she had been fooled by Brody's sweet words and even sweeter kisses.

Sirens sounded in the distance. The police would soon arrive and canvass the neighborhood. What would they find? Nothing to prove any of Brody's suspicions about Ted. In his mind, her brother was the shooter, but Brody was wrong.

So very, very wrong.

Brody appreciated Don Palmer's efforts. The Freemont police chief had pulled in a number of his men to search the Country Club Estates and the surrounding wooded area.

Both Stephanie and Brody had changed back into their street clothes. For the past two hours, she had sat huddled on the couch in the keeping room while the police milled around outside. Fatigue pulled at her drawn face and made him aware of how vulnerable she really was, especially all alone in the big house.

"There's a lodge on post, Stephanie. Why don't you stay there for the next few nights until we find out who fired the shots?"

"What if you don't find the person who's responsible? How long will I have to stay holed up in some motel room?"

"You'll be safer there."

"Chief Palmer said he'd increase patrol cars in the Estates and stationed an officer outside to watch my house."

"For tonight. But what about tomorrow?"

"I'm taking it one day at a time."

He sighed, knowing she wouldn't change her mind.

She picked at a thread on the couch. "I overheard some of the officers talking. One mentioned a hunting area not far from my house, but—"

He waited for her to continue.

"Another one said they found a bullet embedded in one of the posts outside that support the upper deck. It appeared to be the same caliber as used in military rifles."

Was she worried Ted might be involved?

"All military weapons are locked and accounted for in each unit's arms rooms, Stephanie. They're drawn only in certain instances and only with the authorization of the commander."

"So the soldiers don't have access to the rifles?"

"That's right."

"Have you…" She hesitated. "Have you heard back from Major Jenkins?"

He nodded, realizing he should have mentioned the call. "He phoned about thirty minutes ago."

She looked surprised. "Why didn't you tell me?"

"I was outside, talking to the chief at the time. Your brother has been in the barracks all night."

"So he didn't fire the shot."

"Evidently not."

Just because Ted Upton had nothing to do with tonight didn't mean he hadn't caused some of the other problems that had befallen Stephanie over the past few days.

"It's getting late." She stood and rubbed her hands over her arms. "How long before the police leave?"

"They're finishing up now, but I can stay for a while."

"No, Brody. I'll be fine."

He stared long and hard into her eyes. She didn't blink. With a resigned sigh, he grabbed his gym bag and followed her to the door.

"Keep away from the windows," he cautioned. "Don't spend time on your deck or patio. I'll pick you up at seven tomorrow morning for work. Unless that's too early."

"I'll see you then."

Brody hated to leave her, but she needed sleep and he wanted to follow the chief back to police headquarters. Someone had been found about three miles from the Estates, inebriated and talking about his marksmanship. He seemed an unlikely shooter, but he needed to be questioned, and Brody wanted to hear what the guy had to say.

Once outside, he checked that a squad car was in place to watch the Upton house throughout the night. Brody planned to be back after the interrogation, but he needed to know Stephanie would be safe until then.

Before climbing into his car, he turned to look back at the house, wishing he could catch a last glimpse of her. The curtains were drawn. He'd cautioned her to stay away from the windows. This time, Stephanie had taken his advice.

TWELVE

Unable to face Brody, Stephanie called a cab early the next morning. She had slept fitfully, her slumber punctuated with dreams of his strong hands and dark eyes and a horde of police officers that wandered through her yard. She'd awakened with a headache and puffy face from the tears she'd cried before she'd fallen asleep. All the emotion she'd kept bottled up for so long had spilled out as she'd sobbed into her pillow.

The ride to post made her head hurt even more. She blew her nose and applied lipstick before the cab pulled into the WTB area. After paying the driver, she hurried into her office.

By the time the other workers arrived, Stephanie had completed a stack of paperwork that had piled up in her in-box.

A civilian clerk who worked in the records section knocked twice on the door to her office and then entered. With a wide smile, she placed a box of oatmeal-raisin cookies on Stephanie's desk.

"These arrived for you. They're from the Cookie Palace on Fourth Street. They deliver in town and on post."

Stephanie was touched by the thoughtful gesture. "The WTB must have sent them as a welcome gift. I bet Ted told them oatmeal raisin is my favorite type of cookie."

Noticing the clerk's eagerness for her to open the box, Stephanie quickly added, "Are the cookies from you?"

The woman shook her head and pointed to an attached envelope. "The card should tell you who sent them."

Stephanie read the note silently. "Sorry about last night. Brody."

She smiled. "They're from a friend." Evidently he had asked Ted about her preference. Or maybe Nikki.

After removing the outer wrapper, Stephanie handed the box to the other woman. "Would you like to pass them around the office?"

"Don't you want one?" she asked.

"Maybe later."

The clerk returned after a few minutes. "Everyone said to thank you." She placed the remaining cookies on Stephanie's desk and headed back to work.

Unable to resist any longer, Stephanie reached for a particularly large cookie packed with plump raisins. Smiling at Brody's thoughtfulness, she bit into the soft sweetness. Maybe she had reacted too quickly last night.

There was so much she liked about the special agent.

Her office phone rang. She pulled the receiver to

her ear, expecting to hear Brody's voice. Instead, the call was from her regional director.

"Ms. Upton, we've had a complaint from one of the soldiers on your caseload."

Her stomach tightened.

"Private Upton has lodged a formal grievance against you. I'll fax over a list of forms you'll need to fill out. Please return them to me promptly. We take something like this very seriously."

"Yes, sir. I'm not happy about it, either."

When the director hung up, Stephanie dropped her head into her hands. Her cheeks were hot and a bitter taste filled her mouth.

She glanced again at the box of cookies. Surely, they didn't contain peanuts. She was very careful to never eat ones that did, yet the way her throat was feeling, she wondered if she could be having an allergic reaction.

Her skin itched. Looking down, she saw the red rash and patches of hives. Reaching for her cell, she turned on the phone and then hit the saved number for the medical unit attached to the WTB.

"It's Stephanie Upton. I'm sorry to bother you, but…" She struggled to catch her breath. "I'm allergic to peanuts and seem to be having a reaction."

Frustration!

That's what Brody had been feeling since he'd spent the night at police headquarters questioning a number of displaced persons who were wandering the streets of Freemont. One of the police officers had suggested the shooter was some novice outdoorsman who didn't know gun safety or the hunting laws in Georgia. Which Brody didn't buy. Hopefully the chief of police didn't, either.

By the time Brody left P.D. headquarters and arrived at Stephanie's house, she was long gone. Either she had called a cab or driven one of her dad's cars to work. Mad at himself, he had phoned to apologize, but her cell went to voice mail.

Surely, she wasn't rejecting his calls.

He groused the entire drive back to post and was equally frustrated when he was tied up in a meeting that lasted all morning. At lunchtime, he hurried to his car and called her as he neared the WTB.

"I'm sorry I didn't get to your house early enough this morning," he said when she finally answered.

"Don't worry. I took a cab to post, Brody."

"I tried calling you."

"My phone was off. I only realized it a few minutes ago when I phoned my doctor."

Brody spied the ambulance when he turned into the WTB area. He pulled into a parking space, jumped out of his car and ran toward her office.

"What happened?" he said, the phone close to his ear.

She hesitated. "I…I must have had a reaction to the cookies."

A chill settled over him. "What cookies?"

"The note said you were sorry about last night."

He pushed through the door and raced toward her office. Barging into the room, his heart constricted.

She was sitting in a chair with the doctor from the WTB hovering over her, two EMTs at his side.

"Tell me she's okay," he demanded when the doc looked up.

"She's okay. An allergic reaction, but she called us in time."

"In time?"

"She's allergic to peanuts. Evidently, the cookie she ate contained nut particles."

"You didn't know, Brody," she said. Her smile was reassuring, except he was anything but reassured.

"I didn't send you cookies. Someone else must have, but it wasn't me."

Worry flashed from her eyes. "If it wasn't you, then who sent them?"

Someone who knew about Stephanie's allergy. Who would have that type of information?

One person came to mind. Brody fisted his hands. Ted Upton.

"You've had an allergic reaction." Dr. Carter confirmed what the military physician had told Stephanie earlier. Rejecting the EMTs offer to transport her to the Freemont Hospital, she had instead insisted on seeing her family allergist, which the WTB doctor had agreed would be a good idea.

Dr. Carter had treated her mother for years before her death and Stephanie trusted his diagnosis, which was why she had asked Brody to drive her to his office.

"I've only had minor incidents prior to this," Stephanie assured him. "This time I ate an oatmeal-raisin cookie, which shouldn't have peanuts in it, and I had an almost immediate reaction."

"There could have been cross contamination." He glanced at Brody. "You might want to check with the bakery. Sometimes two types of cookies are prepared in the same area. Even a small amount of antigen could cause a reaction."

The doctor turned his gaze back to Stephanie. "As you probably realize by now, allergic reactions are unpredictable. The next one could be minor, but it could also be much more severe. The response might be immediately after you come in contact with the allergen. Then again, you could have a delayed response. I'm telling you this so you don't discount any reaction you might have in the future."

He handed her a prescription. "Get this filled at your pharmacy on the way home. It's for two EpiPen Auto-Injectors, which each contain a single dose of epinephrine. Keep at least one of them with you at all times. You'll find directions printed in the insert."

The doctor glanced at Brody. "If you notice any allergic symptoms, have her use the EpiPen and then be sure to seek medical help. I don't want to scare you, but things can happen quickly once a reaction starts."

The doctor made a note in her file and then patted her arm. "You take after your mother with her big heart. She was a good woman. So are you."

Stephanie's cheeks burned under the doctor's gaze, and knowing Brody was staring at her caused her even more embarrassment.

"I've known your family for years," the doctor

added. "Don't let your concern for Ted keep you from living your own life. He'll find his way. You don't want to miss your own opportunities because you're caring for him."

Stephanie had little to say as Brody drove her to the pharmacy. As much as she appreciated Dr. Carter's advice, she and Ted were a family and needed to stick together. Even if Ted didn't seem to understand what being a family meant.

"That was nice of the doctor to mention your mother," Brody said after they parked and were walking toward the pharmacy. "She must have been a special woman."

Hearing Brody confirm what she already knew made her appreciate him even more. Despite the gun on his hip and his job handling military crime, he had a compassionate side that she had noticed. This was one of those times.

As if he realized her own internal struggle, he circled her with his arm. She leaned into him, supported by his strength.

She shouldn't allow herself to indulge in the moment, but she didn't want to pull back from his closeness. They would separate once they entered the store. Until then, she wanted to pretend they were together and that what they shared was special.

Too soon, she'd have to go back to being the Wounded Warrior advocate and the sister of a soldier who was struggling to find his way. Brody would once again be the CID agent who didn't trust Ted and weighed everything Stephanie said in light of her brother's supposed involvement.

The doctor's words circled through her mind. *You need to live your own life, Stephanie.*

What did she want her own life to entail? At this moment, she wished it included Brody.

Once the prescription was filled and Stephanie had the EpiPens safely tucked in her purse, Brody let out a sigh of relief.

"I'll take you home now," he said.

"I need to go back to work," she insisted. "Keith emailed the report for the island picnic. I have to review his plans and then pass them on to Major Jenkins."

"The major told you to take the afternoon off," Brody reminded her.

"He's been more than kind."

"You've done a great job. Major Jenkins said he can see the strong bonds of trust that you've developed already with the soldiers on your caseload. He also said the class on PTSD had a positive influence, which was good to hear. Since then, a number of the guys have opened up and shared more readily about their own inner struggles."

"Did he mention Ted?"

"Only that he wanted to be removed from your caseload. Jenkins assured him the request would be reviewed, although he hopes to delay the final decision and give you both more time."

"I have a feeling you had something to do with that."

Brody smiled. "I told him you were working to overcome some history that probably played into Ted's current problems. Jenkins suggested I talk to your brother's counselor. I told him you would probably have more information to offer."

She nodded. "I met with his care team and counselor. Ted has been quite reticent about his life before the military. Of course, many soldiers have more than one problem. Often they're dealing with outside issues in addition to their injuries, no matter how traumatic those may be."

"Talking about those other situations helps in the healing process, which I hope Ted realizes." Brody glanced at his watch. "I'm going to have the cookies you received analyzed, but I also want to talk to the folks at the bakery who made them. Do you feel like joining me? If not, I can take you home first."

She smiled. "I told you I need to go back to work, but the bakery isn't far. Nikki Dunn's sister works there. I'm sure Diane can answer any questions you might have. We can stop in and talk to her before we drive back to Fort Rickman."

Brody parked in the small lot behind the bakery. A few people milled about the store when they entered. The smell of freshly baked cookies made his mouth water.

He noticed a sign hanging near the checkout register. "Products containing nuts are made in this facility."

A woman waved to Stephanie. She was in her midthirties and wore a white apron, a hairnet and a warm smile. She bore a striking resemblance to Nikki and was, undoubtedly, the sister Stephanie had mentioned.

The two women embraced before Stephanie introduced him. "Pleasure to meet you, ma'am," he said as they shook hands.

"I placed an order for you this morning."

"Actually, that's why we're here," Brody said. "Could you find the order form?"

Diane rifled through a stack of papers behind the counter. A look of success passed over her face as she pulled one free. "Here it is. Two dozen oatmeal-raisin cookies. The order came in sometime yesterday. Pat was working the counter."

"Is she here today? I'd like to talk to her."

Pat was an older woman with gray hair. Yesterday had been a busy day. She didn't remember anything about the order or the person who had requested the cookies. She apologized for not being able to provide more information before she returned to the kitchen.

Brody briefly mentioned Stephanie's allergic reaction, and then asked Diane, "When was the last time you baked anything containing nuts?"

"Our schedule never varies. We bake sugar and oatmeal in the morning. Chocolate chip, peanut butter and macadamia nut follow. We wipe down the equipment between batches, but a contamination could easily occur. That's why we post the warning." She pointed to the sign Brody had seen upon entering.

"What about your sister, Nikki?" Brody asked. "Does she know the baking schedule?"

"Probably, we haven't changed the routine in years. She used to help out when she was in high school. In fact, Nikki stopped by yesterday with Paul. He bought a dozen macadamia-nut cookies for his mom and dad. They left on a three-day trip this morning."

Diane glanced at Stephanie and lowered her voice. "Truth be told, I'm worried about him. Nikki said he feels guilty. I think it eats at him that his friends were injured."

"Maybe I should encourage Paul to get some help," Stephanie suggested.

As the women talked, Brody peered into the kitchen where Pat was using a large metallic scoop to add an ingredient to the batter she was preparing.

Maybe the problem hadn't been cross contamination.

When he explained his concern to Diane, she ushered him into the kitchen and pointed to the flour and oatmeal bins, and where they kept the other ingredients. Nothing seemed suspect until Brody opened the lid on the raisins. Using a scoop, he sprinkled some on the metal worktable.

Diane gasped.

Brody stared at the tiny particles that appeared to be nuts mixed in with the dried fruit. "I'll need to have this container analyzed. Contact the distributor and see if they've had other complaints."

"Of course. It was probably an error on their part."

"Unless it was done locally by someone who wanted to contaminate your products."

Diane's face paled as she undoubtedly realized the significance of Brody's statement.

"Why?" she asked. "Why would anyone sabotage our bakery?"

Which was exactly the question Brody needed to have answered.

THIRTEEN

To prevent Stephanie from having a second reaction, Brody made her stand back until he placed the container of raisins in his trunk. No doubt, the ground particles were some type of nut. Who had mixed them with the raisins and for what reason was yet to be determined.

Had it been done so that Stephanie would have an allergic reaction? Or was she simply the unsuspecting bystander who happened to get involved? Again the question of coincidence came into play. Too many coincidences didn't add up, especially when they all involved Stephanie.

"I can't understand how nuts could get in with the raisins," Stephanie said as she settled into the passenger seat of Brody's car. "Surely no one would do that on purpose."

"There are sick people in this world with a skewed sense of right and wrong."

"I guess you're right."

Brody rounded the car and climbed behind the wheel.

"Diane mentioned being worried about Paul. Did he and Josh get along?"

"They were always close. I doubt things have changed."

"Unless Paul saw Joshua's injury as too tragic," Brody said. "Some people have flawed ideas about quality of life."

"Josh is the type of guy who makes good things come from whatever life throws his way."

"Yet Paul may not have seen it that way. Did Ted ever give Paul a key to your house?" Brody asked.

"Of course not."

"What about Ted and Nikki? Anything going on between them?"

"They're friends. That's all."

"You said they dated in high school, but Nikki went to prom with Hayden. What about Paul? Did he have a girlfriend?"

"He and Cindy dated."

"Were they serious?"

"About as serious as any seventeen-year-olds can be. They both had a lot of growing up to do."

"Cindy seems to have her feet on the ground now."

Stephanie nodded. "She always knew what she wanted. Money was tight. She didn't go to college. Instead, she helped out with her mom's cleaning service. I'm not sure when she started working for Walt."

Glancing at her watch, Stephanie added, "Since we're not far from the garage, would you mind if we stopped by to see if my car is ready? You've been so kind to chauffer me back and forth to work, but I'm sure you'll be relieved when I get my own car back."

Giving Stephanie rides provided a way to see her and keep her close, which Brody needed to do for the investigation. He also liked being with her.

"We'll check on your car, but you haven't been a burden or a problem. In fact, I've enjoyed our time together."

She hesitated for a moment and looked at him, the sun shining on her hair. "You're very thoughtful, Brody."

Thoughtful? That wasn't what he wanted her to think. He was hoping for a word that was more in keeping with his own feelings, although he'd be hard-pressed to express the way he really felt.

Somehow he got his feelings for Stephanie mixed up with his memory of Lisa. Yet Stephanie was different. She was here, and Lisa was gone.

Instead of dreaming about Lisa as he'd done for so long, he had started to dream about Stephanie and that had him wondering about this investigation.

He was reacting like someone who was too involved, too committed. Not to the case, but to Stephanie.

"The tires came in yesterday," Walt told Stephanie once she and Brody arrived at the garage. "I meant to call you."

The cost of the four tires would put a significant hole in her bank account, which was one of the reasons Stephanie was glad she could live at home, at least until she received her first paycheck.

"Where's the car?" Brody asked after she paid the bill.

Walt handed her the keys and pointed behind the garage. "It's parked out back."

"My radar for danger is picking up bad vibes," Brody said as he and Stephanie rounded the garage. Her Corolla was parked next to a wooded area well away from the street. "I'm glad you didn't come here at night alone."

She shook her head, somewhat amused. "Do you CID guys always imagine the worst-case scenario?"

He raised his brow and held up four fingers. "Joshua Webb was attacked. Your house was broken into and a warning left. A bridge collapsed with you on it. You were almost shot." He raised his thumb. "Should we add the mysterious cookie delivery?"

She held up her hand to stop him. "It's daytime. You're with me, and the car looks fine."

"I'll follow you back to post."

"I usually take the two lane through town that runs along the river."

"Got it. The scenic route. But I'm still following you."

He helped her into her car and waited until she started the engine before he climbed behind the wheel of his own car. Stephanie hummed a tune as she pulled out of the parking space and headed along the winding River Road.

The sun was shining and warmed the day. Stephanie turned up the air conditioner and appreciated the coolness that soon circulated through the car. Glancing repeatedly at her rearview mirror, she watched for Brody's car to appear.

As much as she liked having her Corolla back, she had enjoyed having a reason to see Brody. Hopefully, they'd continue to get together. Maybe he could schedule another class for the WTB. She'd call him once she was back at her desk and see what they could arrange.

A sharp curve appeared ahead. A sign on the side of the road warned trucks to apply their brakes. She glanced at her speedometer and, realizing she was going faster than the limit, tapped the brakes.

Instead of slowing down, the car gained momentum. She pressed down harder on the brake pedal and swallowed a ball of anxiety that climbed into her throat.

Gripping the steering wheel with one hand, she downshifted with the other. The vehicle shuddered and the speed dropped ever so slightly, but once she entered the curve, she struggled to keep the wheels on the road.

The steep downward slope of the roadway ahead made her stomach roil. A huge semi tractor-trailer chugged up the hill in the opposite lane. She flashed her lights to signal her distress.

The trucker flashed back, no doubt oblivious to her need.

She glanced again at the speedometer. Seventy miles per hour. Too fast.

Bile soured her stomach.

If Brody were behind the wheel, he'd know what to do.

Think. Think.

The semi neared. She held her breath. The trucker blew his horn as she whizzed past him.

A straight stretch of roadway lay ahead, flanked by thick woods to the left and a five-foot drop-off to the river on the right.

She tramped on the emergency-brake pedal. The car slowed ever so slightly before accelerating once again.

A sports utility vehicle approached.

A woman sat at the wheel with three little heads perched in car seats behind her.

Stephanie's car shimmied out of control and swerved into the left lane. She tugged on the steering wheel, nearly sideswiping the SUV before she lost control. The Corolla crossed the right-hand lane, jumped the curb and slid down the hill.

Her heart lodged in her throat.

The last thing she heard was the name she screamed. "Brody!"

Brody increased his speed, needing to catch up with Stephanie. A series of red lights had delayed him in town. Now on the open roadway, he hoped to make up time.

He spied her car rounding a curve up ahead.

His heart lurched. She was going fast. Too fast.

He raced forward.

God, help her. The internal prayer came without forethought.

He pushed down on the accelerator and took the curve at a fast rate. His own heart beat wildly as a huge semi rolled past him, followed by an SUV.

Searching the distance, Brody saw only the empty road. Where was she?

A swirl of dust caught his eye.

His gut tightened.

"Stephanie," he screamed.

Screeching to a stop, he punched nine-one-one on his cell and sprang from his car, relaying information to the operator.

"Send an ambulance and medical responders now."

He stumbled down the hill toward where her car had landed on its side. The engine still purred. Peering through the front windshield, he saw Stephanie suspended by her seat belt, the airbag limp around her. Her eyes were closed, her cheek bloodied. Her tousled hair dangled in the air.

He climbed the hood and yanked on the door.

The latch held. Pounding on the driver's window, he screamed her name.

Another fear rose up within him, more deadly than the crash.

Smoke.

If he didn't get Stephanie out, she would be trapped inside the car as it went up in flames.

A voice penetrated the darkness.

Stephanie moaned.

Her body ached. A jackhammer pounded through her brain.

She wanted to slip back into the darkness.

"Stephanie."

Insistent. Pleading.

She recognized the voice.

"Br...Brody?"

More pounding.

"Open your eyes, Stephanie. The door's locked. Release the latch."

She blinked against the light, feeling a swell of nausea. The world hung topsy-turvy around her.

She tried to make sense of the disorder. The only constant was Brody's voice.

Turning her head ever so slightly, she saw his face pressed against the window, his palm pounding against the glass.

"Unlock the door," he screamed.

Lifting her left hand, she flipped the small knob on the door handle.

Smoke swirled around her.

Instinctively, she cowered.

The door opened. With a snap, Brody released the seat belt, grabbed her purse and lifted her into his arms.

Holding her close, he jumped to the ground below.

"Brody," she whispered, wanting to drift away from the chaos.

"Don't leave me, honey."

The acrid smell of smoke and fuel filled her nostrils. Blinking open her eyes, she turned her head ever so slightly, seeing flames shoot skyward.

Sirens sounded in the distance.

Everything seemed surreal except the pounding of Brody's heart and his pull of air as he carried her away from the carnage, away from the fire, away from danger.

* * *

Brody hovered next to the EMTs as they worked on Stephanie. A bandage covered the cut on her forehead. The blood had been cleaned from her face, but she still looked pale, which worried him.

One of the EMTs stood. "Can you give us a little room, sir?"

Stephanie glanced up at Brody and smiled, not quite a full grin but enough to reassure him.

"How's the injury to her head?" he asked.

"Looks like she's going to be okay, sir. We're taking her to the local hospital. You can follow us there."

"I'll ride with her in the ambulance."

"Brody, I'm all right." Stephanie tried to reassure him. "Drive your own car. We'll both need a ride home from the hospital."

She was thinking more soundly than he was at this point.

Brody turned to the EMT. "Are you sure she can make the trip?"

"She seems in good shape," the EMT said. "But we want the E.R. doc to check her out first. You understand?"

Brody understood the EMT, but not what had happened.

He glanced at the smoldering pile of twisted metal that had been Stephanie's car.

The Freemont chief of police stood near the wreckage. Brody approached Palmer.

"Any idea what happened?" Brody asked.

"She was going too fast, for sure. She said the

brakes didn't work. We'll check out what's left of the vehicle, but it's doubtful we'll ever pinpoint what malfunctioned. If there was evidence, it probably burned up in the fire."

"Did you send someone to talk to Walt at the garage?"

"He wasn't there, but his sister was more than helpful. They've had some problem with vandalism over the past few weeks. We picked up a couple of teenagers last week. They denied everything, but we're pretty sure they're involved. I'm sending someone to bring them back in for questioning."

"Why would they tamper with Stephanie's brakes?"

"Beats me." Palmer scratched his chin. "A lot has happened to Ms. Upton. Are you sure she wouldn't do something like this to attract attention to herself?"

"That's ridiculous. She came back to this area to help her brother. He's the one with the problem. I need to find out if anyone saw him around the garage."

"I talked to Major Jenkins. Private Upton's been in his barracks." He flicked his gaze to Stephanie. "You know very well that some folks make up stories to be the center of attention. Stephanie's mama died young. Her daddy is a workaholic who never gave the kids enough of his time. Now her brother's a war hero." The cop continued. "It's a possibility she needed to feel wanted or protected or important. Maybe all three. Wasn't that long ago when Stephanie Upton was one of the young women to watch in this area. Folks thought she'd do well in life."

Success wasn't important. Staying alive was.

"She *has* done well," Brody countered. "She's got a good job on post and is an effective and compassionate advocate for wounded soldiers. That's something to admire, in my opinion."

"I agree." Palmer patted Brody's shoulder. "Just keep an open mind. Sometimes there's more than one way to look at a situation."

"What about Joshua? She saved his life."

"Ms. Upton was the first on the scene. Does that tell you anything?"

It meant she could have staged the attack to look like an accident, which Brody had first considered but soon discarded after talking to Stephanie at Josh's house.

"The shot last night wasn't her imagination."

Palmer nodded. "I agree, but other things have happened."

Brody thought of the bull's-eye on the photograph in her kitchen and on her bedsheets, as well as the collapsed bridge. So far he hadn't discussed the allergic reaction with the chief. He'd save that for later, once he knew for sure what was mixed with the raisins. No reason at the present moment to add more fuel to the fire.

Glancing at the burning embers of what had been Stephanie's car, Brody knew the chief had enough suspicions of his own.

Brody didn't want to hear anything negative about Stephanie. She wouldn't have attacked Joshua or purposefully crashed her car.

Looking at where Stephanie lay brought back memories of Lisa.

The pain of loss twisted his gut. Lisa had been murdered by a killer no one suspected, least of all Brody.

If only he had put the warning signs together that were so evident in hindsight.

What sign was he missing now?

He thought of everything that had happened as he followed the ambulance to the hospital. The paramedics wheeled Stephanie into the E.R., where a competent team of medical personnel rushed her into the treatment room. He paced the hallway until the doctor opened the door and announced she could go home.

Relief swept over Brody, replacing the oppressive heaviness that had surrounded him since the accident.

He couldn't help but smile as he stepped into the trauma room.

She sat on the edge of the stretcher. Without saying a word, she reached for him.

He wrapped his arms around her. A surge of joy coursed through him. He buried his head in her hair. Despite what she'd been through, he could smell the scent of her shampoo mixed with the smoke that lingered on both of them.

"Thank you," she whispered. "If you hadn't followed me…"

"I should have gotten there sooner."

"You saved me, Brody. You saved my life."

He knew what could have happened. The thought made him hold her even more closely.

"No matter how hard I stepped on the brake, the car didn't respond." She shook her head. "There was a truck and then an SUV with kids in the back."

"It's okay, hon. You don't need to think about it now."

"But if something else had happened—"

She didn't finish the thought.

Brody told her about the teen vandals and the chief of police's concern that they could have been the perpetrators.

"I'm surprised you don't suspect Ted," she said at last.

"He's been in the barracks, Stephanie. Ted wasn't involved."

She nodded, appreciation evident in her gaze. "At least, we agree on that."

"Let's go." He grabbed her hand and hurried her out of the E.R. "I'm taking you someplace safe."

FOURTEEN

Brody held the door open to his bachelor officer's quarters on post.

"Your apartment's lovely," Stephanie said as she walked through the doorway. Brody watched as she glanced around the room, taking in the overstuffed couch and chair, the plasma-screen television and speakers and the bistro table with four chairs and serving sideboard.

He had decorated the living area in earth tones, pulled together with an Oriental rug, which her surprised expression said she hadn't expected.

Her eyes widened with appreciation as she stepped toward a group of framed charcoal sketches that decorated the walls, all desert scenes of stark hills and big boulders piled next to a two-lane road that cut through the wilderness.

"They're beautiful, Brody."

Her gaze dropped to the artist's name. Goodman. She turned. "Someone in your family?"

He smiled. "I'm glad you like them."

"Your mother? Father? Grandfather?" She glanced

at the next sketch, again pointing to the Goodman name. "Who's the artist?"

"They're mine. I started drawing to pass the time in Afghanistan. The sketches you see here are from Fort Irwin, in the Mojave Desert, where I was stationed following my first deployment."

One sketch was of a noble mountain outlined against the desert terrain, the sun setting behind the peak. In the distance, the vast arid terrain stretched barren and lonely.

"The stark surroundings are haunting," she said. "Barren. Lonely. They remind me of a time in my life shortly after I left Freemont. I missed my home and my brother."

Brody moved toward her and wrapped his arm around her shoulder as they both stared at the drawings. "I sketched those pictures when I was a young soldier. The army had provided a way for me to make something better than the path I was on back in L.A. My family had problems." He shrugged. "I guess a lot of families do."

Stephanie nodded as if she understood. "What are you working on now?"

He shook his head. "I haven't sketched anything in years."

"Because—"

He let out a deep breath, knowing he needed to share the past with Stephanie. Maybe then she would understand his concern about Ted.

"A girl from home came to visit me about the time I sketched these drawings. She had written me during my first deployment, and I wanted a nice place for her to stay. I didn't have a car. Barstow was the closest town, and it was more than a thirty-mile drive from post through the desert."

Stephanie pointed to the picture of the two-lane road, cutting across the stark terrain. "What you've sketched here."

He nodded. "My first sergeant's wife was a jewel. She had a heart as big as Texas, where she and the Sarge were from originally. She invited Lisa to stay with her."

Stephanie tilted her head, no doubt hearing the pain in his voice.

"Sarge seemed like a good guy. No one realized he was having problems. Trouble sleeping. Bouts of rage. That night..."

Brody turned, not wanting to continue.

"You told the soldiers that it helps to talk about situations in the past." Stephanie touched his shoulder and hesitated a moment before asking, "What happened, Brody?"

He rubbed his hand over his jaw. "They pieced it together. Sarge must have had an episode that night. He killed his wife. He killed Lisa, too, and then he killed himself."

Stephanie wrapped her arms around him.

"I was the first one at the scene the next morning."

"Oh, Brody, I'm so sorry."

"That's why I worry about Ted. No one knew about Sarge's outrages. Looking back, it's easy to see he was probably suffering from PTSD."

He turned to stare into her crystal-clear eyes. "I can't protect you all the time, and that's what scares me. You've got to protect yourself when it comes to your brother."

"But I can't turn my back on Ted."

He had to show her how he felt. Staring down at her parted lips, he sensed the swell of emotion that coursed between them. He didn't want to think about the past—not his or hers. He just wanted to think about the present moment and how much he cared about her.

She looked at him expectantly, and then rose on tiptoe. He lowered his mouth, tasting the sweetness of his lips.

He raked his hands through her hair and pulled her even closer. The swell of his own heart seemed to explode within him; suddenly he wasn't alone anymore, and everything that mattered was in his arms.

At that moment, her phone chirped.

She pulled back ever so slightly. Regret wrapped around her pretty face. Her cheeks flushed, and she pushed her hands against his chest, needing space, which he gave her, feeling an instant sense of loss.

She searched in her purse and raised the cell to her ear.

"Ted? You heard about the accident." She looked relieved. "I'm okay. My car was totaled, but I wasn't hurt."

Brody stared at the painting of the lonely desert landscape. Stephanie would always put Ted first. Selfish as it may seem, he didn't want to be second-best, not when it came to a lifetime commitment.

But then he was getting ahead of himself and his relationship with Stephanie. If there even was a relationship.

He'd been alone for so long. Now that Stephanie was in his life, he didn't want to let her go.

Brody fixed Stephanie a sandwich with chips and insisted she relax on the couch while he headed to his home office in the spare bedroom.

The first call he made was to his boss at CID headquarters. He filled Chief Wilson in on what had happened.

"Do you think her brake problem is random?" Wilson asked.

"I don't know what to think, sir. The Freemont chief of police mentioned vandalism in that area of town. I'm going to call the garage and see what the owner has to say."

"Walt's worked on my car a number of times. He runs a good business, but looks can be deceiving."

Which brought to mind the police chief's concern about Stephanie wanting to be the center of attention. Brody saw no reason to relay Palmer's suspicions.

"A lot has happened to Ms. Upton," the chief mused.

"Yes, sir."

"Make sure nothing else does, will you, Brody?"

"That's my goal, sir."

"See what you can find out today and brief me in the morning."

"Will do, sir."

He disconnected and dialed Ferrol's Garage. Walt

answered with a curt greeting and quickly answered Brody's questions about the vandalism problem the local area had been having.

"As I told the police, the kids have done some pranks, but nothing as significant as this. Although Stephanie's car was an older model, I had it humming like a baby when I signed off on the work order."

"Someone could have tampered with the brakes either in your garage or when it was parked out back."

"Whoa there, Mr. Special Agent. You're jumping to the wrong conclusion and getting me riled up, to boot. I stand by my work. I wouldn't do anything to cause a problem."

"Then who did?"

"Exactly what I've been trying to find out. I just checked online for any recalls on that make and model. A couple years back, there had been a number of cases of brake failure. Stands to reason that could have been Stephanie's problem."

"Wouldn't she have been notified?" Brody asked.

"If she bought the car used, the recall notice may have been sent to the original owner or lost in the mail. Everything looked good when I was under the hood. No telling what malfunctioned."

"Do me a favor and call the chief of police and let him know what you told me."

"Will do."

Brody's next call was to the hospital for an update on Joshua's condition. The news wasn't good.

He disconnected and headed to the living room, where he found Stephanie asleep on the couch. He stood for a long moment, staring down at her, wishing things could be different. If only she trusted him. Together they'd be able to help Ted, Brody felt sure.

But she didn't want him involved.

He touched her shoulder. "Stephanie?"

She opened her eyes, then smiled. Her lips were puffy with sleep and so inviting. His chest tightened as he realized how strong his feelings were for her.

"Joshua's taken a turn for the worse," Brody said. "I'm gong to the hospital."

Stephanie sat up and glanced around his BOQ. "Point me to your restroom so I can comb my hair and freshen my lipstick. I want to go with you."

She returned quickly, all hint of her sleepiness gone. He grabbed her hand and together they hurried to his car.

"I'll call Major Jenkins and alert him," Stephanie said. "Joshua's parents need to be notified, as well as the WTB chaplain."

She'd completed the calls by the time Brody parked at the hospital. He placed his hand protectively on her back as they rode the elevators to the ICU.

"We're here to see PFC Joshua Webb," Brody said as they approached the nurse's station and flashed his CID identification.

Stephanie's grip on Brody's hand tightened when they stepped into the small room. Joshua's face was pale as death. An IV bag dripped medication ever so slowly into his vein. If only it would combat the infection that was running rampant through his body.

"Josh, it's Stephanie." She touched his feverish arm.

"Special Agent Goodman is here with me. Remember he visited you in the hospital earlier?"

"Good to see you, Joshua."

Stephanie smiled at Joshua, but her eyes were filled with concern. She patted his arm. "Don't worry about anything, except getting better. When you're stronger, we'll take you to your house. A local group of businessmen want to help with the renovations."

The soldier's lips moved ever so slightly.

The WTB chaplain, a tall lieutenant colonel with a long face and compassionate eyes, entered the room. He nodded to Stephanie and Brody before he approached the head of the bed and bent down to talk with Josh.

Brody and Stephanie stepped back to give them privacy.

After a few minutes, the chaplain motioned them forward. "Would you join me in prayer?"

Stephanie folded her hands and bowed her head. Standing next to her, Brody did the same.

"Dear Lord," the chaplain began, his voice strong and determined. "We call upon You in this time of need, and ask Your help to bring Joshua through this illness. He is Your child, and we know Your love for him surpasses any human love. You want the very best for Josh, and we're confident that, at this moment, You are surrounding him with Your love and mercy. Fill his heart with love for You, Lord. Help the doctors and nurses who care for him, and allow the medication to be effective to combat the infection. We ask for renewed strength for Joshua as he places his trust in You. For this we pray, amen."

Before the minister had opened his eyes, a scuffle sounded in the hallway. Stephanie turned to see Ted standing in the doorway. His face was filled with pain.

He glanced at Stephanie. "You...you didn't tell me he was in such bad shape."

"I didn't know until just a short while ago."

Tears swam in Ted's eyes. "You called the chaplain, but you didn't call me. My squad leader told me the news."

Ted's world was caving in around him once again. Another person in his life was being taken for him. The look on his face showed too clearly the knife that had lodged in his heart.

He took a step back to where Paul stood, his face pale, his eyes wide as if he, too, was struggling with a wave of emotions he couldn't handle.

"It's just like it was when Mom died, isn't it, Stephanie?" Ted said. "You didn't let me know. You and Dad kept it from me. Yet I was the one who had been with her through it all while you stayed at college."

"Which is what Mom wanted, Ted." Her voice was low and filled with compassion. Why did he fail to remember her repeated requests to stay home that semester? "I did what Mom wanted."

"You keep telling me that, but it's not true. You did what you wanted, and then at the end, you were the one standing at her bedside. You let her die without calling me."

"I called the school and told them you needed to come home. Aunt Hazel picked you up."

"Too late. I was too late."

"Mom was still alive when you got home, Ted. But you refused to see her."

He shook his head. "You're lying."

He turned and ran from the ICU.

"Ted!" Stephanie ran after him.

He opened the door to the stairwell and raced down the steps.

She followed, calling his name. "Ted, stop."

The outside door on the first floor opened. She ran even faster, her feet tripping down the stairs. She had to reach him, but when she stepped into the hot afternoon, he was nowhere to be seen.

She had called the high school that day to notify the school that Aunt Hazel was coming to pick up her brother. The secretary had trouble locating him, and when Ted arrived home, their mother's breathing was labored. Knowing she didn't have much time, Stephanie had encouraged Ted to go to her bedside. He had balked. The pain of seeing their mother moving from this life to the next was too hard for him.

Ted remembered what he thought had happened, but it was far from the truth. If only he could see the past with clarity. She needed to, as well. Maybe then, she'd stop blaming herself for everything that had gone wrong.

FIFTEEN

"Direct me," Brody said to Stephanie once they were in his car again. "Where would Ted go when he's upset?"

"Maybe the cemetery where my mother's buried. He might go to her grave site."

On the way off post, she called Paul, but his phone went immediately to voice mail. She called Nikki next, who didn't know about Joshua's decline. Nor did she know anything about Ted.

"Phone me if he contacts you," Stephanie said before she disconnected.

Brody saw the worry weighing down her shoulders. "What about Cindy? Would your brother contact her?"

"I'll try her cell." Stephanie pulled the number from her contacts file and paused before she looked at Brody. "It's going to voice mail."

She left a message while Brody called the garage. Walt answered.

"Stephanie needs to talk to your sister," Brody told him. "Could you put her on?"

"She's helping our mom with her cleaning business this afternoon. Anything I can pass along?"

Brody explained about the decline in Joshua's condition and Ted's reaction. "If Cindy runs into Ted, have her call Stephanie."

"That boy's had a lot of loss in his short life. 'Spect seeing his buddy in such bad shape is eating at him. What about Paul? He might know something."

"They're together. Stephanie's trying to reach Paul now."

Eventually, Paul answered his cell, but he refused to let Stephanie talk to Ted. From the one-sided conversation Brody heard, Paul was struggling as much as her brother.

Stephanie filled Brody in on their conversation once she disconnected. "He talked about Joshua not wanting to live since the amputation, but Paul's wrong. Josh has always been optimistic about the future, and from what everyone at the WTB has told me, his outlook never changed, even after he lost his legs. Paul's transferring his own feelings onto Josh, which concerns me. I offered to schedule an appointment for Paul with one of the social workers. I told him talking about his feelings would help."

"Did he agree to see someone?"

"Yes, although he didn't seem too enthused."

She called the mental-health office on post and gave the receptionist Paul's name. "They'll squeeze him in tomorrow afternoon," she told Brody.

When she called Paul back, he failed to answer once again. She left the information about his appointment in a voice mail before she disconnected.

Once they turned into the cemetery, her outward

demeanor changed. Brody could see the pain in her gaze as he parked by a small knoll near a number of grave sites. Without speaking, she exited the car and walked slowly to a granite marker. Brody stood back, giving her space and privacy.

He studied the surrounding hills and manicured grounds, looking for any sign of Ted or Paul. The sun beat down overhead, causing sweat to dampen his neck.

Stephanie retraced her steps, her gaze sweeping the area. "I had hoped Ted would be here."

"Where else would he go?"

She shook her head. "Maybe back to our house."

They drove in silence, the heaviness of seeing her mother's grave evident in the slump of her shoulders and the way she toyed with her watch.

Brody longed to pull to the side of the road and wrap her in his arms, but she was focused on Ted and the past and the pain that she and her brother still carried.

Arriving at her house, he walked her to the porch where he waited until she had unlocked the door and disengaged the security alarm.

"I know you won't change the locks, Stephanie, but you could change the alarm on your own. The owner's manual will explain what you need to do. It just means plugging in another code. I'll help you."

When she hesitated, he added, "You didn't think Ted was in the house the other night, and if he wasn't, then someone else was here. Let me walk you through the steps."

"What if Ted comes back?"

"You'll hear him at the door. That shouldn't be a problem."

She let out a long sigh. "Maybe you're right. I'd probably sleep better."

She looked tired and worried.

He helped her reprogram the alarm and turned his back when she entered the new four-digit code.

"You can watch, Brody. I trust you."

He shook his head. "I want you to be the only one who knows this code."

Once the alarm was reprogrammed, they headed into the kitchen. "Grab some water from the bottom shelf in the refrigerator," Stephanie said. "I'll check the phone for messages."

A sound on the front porch caused them both to pause.

A key turned in the lock.

"It's Ted." Stephanie hurried into the foyer.

The front door opened just as Brody caught up to her.

Ted's eyes widened as he looked from Stephanie to Brody. "What's he doing here?"

The security system beeped. Ted tapped in the code. The old code.

Brody anticipated the scream of the alarm seconds before the system activated.

The deafening screech filled the house.

Ted stepped back, his face awash with disbelief and pain. "You changed the code, didn't you?" He pointed to Brody. "It's because of him. He convinced you I'm dangerous. That I'm crazy. That I could hurt you."

"Ted, please," she pleaded.

"You had a decision to make, didn't you, Stephanie? You could trust me or him. You chose him." Ted ran from the house and into the night.

Brody chased after him, but lost sight of Ted in the woods at the rear of the property. He returned to the house just as Stephanie backed her father's Cadillac out of the garage.

"What are you doing?"

"I'm going after him, Brody. You're still living in the past. I'm not Lisa, and my brother isn't the sergeant that killed her. You made me change the alarm, but I can't do things your way anymore. I transferred to Fort Rickman to help Ted. He's my responsibility."

"Stephanie, please."

"I've got to do this on my own. Don't follow me, Brody."

"I want to help you."

"You've done too much already. Stay away from me, and stay away from my brother."

Stephanie raced out of the driveway and through the Estates until she arrived at Paul's house. She pulled to the curb in front of the three-story structure that was far larger than the Upton home. The grounds were perfectly manicured and decorated with flower gardens and clusters of ornamental trees. In the daylight, the home was a showplace, but tonight it sat dark and foreboding.

She ran up the walk and climbed the steps to the

porch. Not wanting to waste time with the bell, she pounded on the door.

"I'm coming," Paul's voice sounded from inside the house. Hopefully, she'd find Ted inside and be able to explain what had happened.

Paul's surprise at seeing her was evident when he opened the door. "I dropped Ted off at your house, Stephanie, not more than ten minutes ago."

"He ran away from me, Paul. Where would go?"

"The Italian Parlor isn't far, especially if he takes the shortcut across the golf course. You might try there."

She hurried back to her car. Paul was right. The pizza parlor was a favorite spot for many of the local kids and an easy hike using the golf-cart paths and nature trails. By road, the trip took longer, but she eventually pulled into the parking lot and raced inside, hit by the pungent aroma of freshly baked pizza. Bowls of peanuts sat on each table, the discarded shells scattered on the floor.

Careful to stay clear of the debris lest she have an allergic reaction, Stephanie scanned the tables and quickly spied Nikki. A guy sat across from her in the booth, his back to the door. They turned as she neared.

"Keith?"

He smiled sheepishly while Nikki held up an open folder. "We're going over the plans for the Wounded Warrior picnic," she said.

Keith nodded a bit too quickly. "I wanted Nikki to review everything before I gave you the final copy."

"You already submitted the plans," Stephanie said.

"Those were tentative." He placed a second folder,

containing about ten pages of typed notes, on the table in front of her and tapped it twice with his hand. "You'll find everything in here. Let me know if you want me to change anything."

She appreciated the work he had done on the project. He seemed to be genuinely concerned about the military and eager that the picnic be a special day for the soldiers. Maybe she had underestimated her cousin.

"Have either of you seen Ted?"

Nikki nodded. "He was here a few minutes ago, out of breath and saying he needed wheels."

"I volunteered to drive Nikki home," Keith said. "Which solved his transportation problem. He left in Nikki's car not more than three minutes ago."

"Do you know where he was headed?"

Keith shrugged. "He didn't say."

"But he did tell us Josh wasn't doing well and asked me to pray for him," Nikki shared.

"Really?"

The younger woman nodded. "His squad leader's been talking to him about God and how much He loves us. Ted's never been much of a believer, but he's been listening. I guess some of it rubbed off."

Stephanie remembered going to church regularly with her mother when she was young. They would sit with Aunt Hazel and Keith. All that changed after Ted was born.

"He also mentioned wanting to visit Keith's mom," Nikki continued. "Ted said he hadn't seen her since he left for Afghanistan."

After bidding them a hasty farewell, Stephanie returned to her dad's car and drove toward Magnolia Gardens Nursing Home. The facility sat along a narrow two-lane road on the outskirts of town.

Pulling into the parking lot, she rubbed her free hand over her stomach in an attempt to calm her agitation. She wasn't ready to face Aunt Hazel, but she needed to find Ted.

Hurrying inside, she approached the receptionist, who pointed her down the hall. "Hazel Allen's room is 110, the sixth door on the left."

Stephanie's footfalls clipped over the tile floor and kept time with the thumping of her heart. She hadn't seen Nikki's car in the front lot, but additional spaces were available in the rear, where Ted could have parked.

Stopping outside room 110, she gazed at the sleeping woman who reminded her so much of her own mother. Hazel had the same high cheekbones and warm smile, and even from this distance, Stephanie was struck by the resemblance.

As much as she wanted to draw closer, she didn't have time. If Ted wasn't with Aunt Hazel, where could he be?

Driving back to town, Stephanie felt an added weight pulling her down. Her brother had to feel rejected and pushed aside, unwelcome even in his own home, which wasn't the case, of course.

Brody's rationale for changing the security code had seemed logical at the time. She never thought how it would affect Ted until the alarm sounded. The sense of betrayal that played across his face revealed the depth of his pain.

Stephanie would give anything to change what had happened, just as she wanted to change that afternoon on the lake. If only mistakes could be corrected with a wave of the hand. Instead, they often festered, causing long-term pain and deep divides that tore families apart.

Arriving back in town, Stephanie headed toward the town square. On the way, she passed the brick church on the corner of Freemont Road and Third Street. Surrounding the church were a number of alleyways where the congregation parked on Sunday mornings. Stephanie didn't want to lose precious time circling the neighborhood in hopes of spotting Nikki's car. Instead, she pulled to the curb and hurried toward the church.

Pulling open the massive door, she stared into the dimly lit sanctuary and empty pews. An overwhelming need to talk to the Lord drew her forward. She walked down the center aisle and slipped into the front pew.

Brass candelabra graced the oak altar, which was draped with a linen cloth. Although the candles weren't lit, the smell of beeswax hung in the church like a sacred scent, bringing back memories of services in her youth.

In the stillness, she remembered her mother's laughter, the sound like music that made tears stream from her eyes.

"I tried to love him like you did, Mama." Stephanie dropped her head into her hands. "I wanted to fill the hole in my own heart, but even more so, I wanted to knit together his brokenness. I…I tried to be you." She swiped her hand across her cheeks. "Ted didn't want me. He needed you and Dad, but you know how that went. I thought Dad might change after…after your death. But he'll never change, I finally realized."

Her own voice broke as she thought back to her mother's funeral and then Hayden's.

"I'm…I'm sorry for what I did. For my anger at Ted. For waiting too long and for not getting there in time."

Stephanie shook her head. She couldn't let her brother down again. His well-being depended on her just as it had three years ago. Regretting the mistake she had made then, she had to find Ted. Not knowing where to turn, she turned to the Lord.

Dear God, I feel so hopelessly lost. Help me find my brother.

SIXTEEN

Driving back to town, Brody called the Warrior Transitional Battalion, hoping Ted had returned to his barracks. The squad leader had questioned Ted's roommate and others on his floor, but no one had heard from him.

The second call was to the chief of police. Brody filled him in on what had happened. "If anything develops, call me."

"Anything meaning what?" Palmer asked.

"A vehicular accident, a soldier walking alone along the river or getting drunk at some hole-in-the-wall bar. Ted Upton shows symptoms of PTSD. He's balanced on a tightrope that could be dangerous to himself or someone else. Just tell your officers on patrol to keep their eyes open."

Brody also informed CID headquarters and the military police on post. He wanted to be proactive and ensure Ted's situation didn't become more severe. And he didn't want anyone else hurt.

Stephanie's bitter words played over in his head. She didn't want him interfering with her brother, but she failed to realize the terrible consequences of what could happen.

Once again, he recalled the carnage, and Lisa's body lying in a pool of blood. Tonight that memory seemed so raw.

Then, instead of Lisa, he saw Stephanie with her blue eyes, the color of a clear sky on a summer's day, and her hair like stands of silk that caressed his cheek when he held her close, which is what he wanted to do now.

His cell rang. He grabbed it from the console. "Special Agent Goodman."

"Sir, this is Sergeant McCoy from the WTB."

Ted's squad leader. Brody felt a surge of euphoria. "Did PFC Upton return to the barracks?"

"Negative, sir, but the guys said he likes the Italian Parlor in town. This time of night, he often stops in for pizza and a couple of beers."

"Bowls of roasted peanuts on the tables?"

"That's the place." The squad leader gave Brody directions.

Pulling into the parking lot, Brody spied Keith and Nikki leaving the restaurant.

Rolling down his window, he quickly asked about Ted.

"Stephanie stopped by right after Ted left," Keith said. "She may have gone to the nursing home. It's located north along the Freemont Road."

He handed Brody a manila folder. "She left in a hurry and forgot to take this file on the Wounded Warrior picnic. You'll see her before I will."

With a quick thank-you and a sigh of relief, Brody tossed the folder on the passenger's seat and then increased his speed as he headed toward the nursing home. Halfway through town, he spotted the Uptons' Cadillac parked in front of a small, brick church on Third Street and pulled into the parking lot.

Taking the steps two at a time, he raced inside, overcome with relief when he saw Stephanie sitting in the front. Unwilling to interrupt her conversation with the Lord, he stood shadowed in the rear and watched as she heaved herself up from the pew and turned toward the door.

If only she would accept his help. Almost afraid of what she would say, Brody pulled in a deep breath and stepped into the light.

She gasped. Her hand clutched her throat. "Were you watching me?"

"I was waiting until you stopped praying. I want to help you find Ted."

He could see the tears that filled her eyes and the puffy redness to her cheeks even in the half light.

She shook her head. "I told you, I have to do this alone."

"I'll follow you, just to keep you safe."

"Didn't you hear me earlier? I'm not Lisa."

Of course, she wasn't Lisa. Lisa had been gone for so long that he hardly remembered what she looked like. Stephanie was real and warm and sweet and soft every place she should be, and being with her made Brody feel whole again for the first time in so very long.

"I'm worried about your brother and his safety, but I'm also worried about you." He hoped she heard the sincerity in his voice. "I can't separate the way I feel about you from the job I do in the military, a job that is at the heart of who I am, Stephanie. I won't get in your way unless you're in danger."

The look on her face told him she was softening. He remembered what he and his friends had said when they were kids.

"I won't get in your way," he repeated. "Cross my heart." He raised his right hand and made a small cross over his heart. The childlike promise took on a new meaning in the church with the larger cross hanging behind the altar.

His heart had opened somewhat to the Lord, but he wasn't willing to put Stephanie's safety solely in God's hands. He needed to be with her to ensure she wasn't in harm's way.

She didn't have a choice. Neither did he.

Brody would die himself rather than let anything happen to Stephanie. He'd made a horrific mistake with Lisa. She was in the past, but he wouldn't make a second mistake that would cause another woman to lose her life.

Especially when that woman was Stephanie.

A woman he now realized he loved.

Stephanie glanced into her rearview mirror and spied Brody's headlights. True to his word, he'd followed her as she had driven through town looking for her brother. He had also alerted the military police who were searching for Ted on post.

Brody assured her law enforcement wouldn't do anything to threaten Ted or cause his fragile mental health harm. She'd already done enough by changing the security code.

She shouldn't have listened to Brody. Not long ago, she had hoped something might develop between them, especially in the weeks to come, when Ted's condition improved.

How silly to think anything good could come from knowing Brody.

He saw everyone—especially her brother—as a threat. Stephanie wanted to heal Ted's pain and help him move forward. Her brother and Brody were polar opposites that would never be reconciled. No matter how much she was attracted to Brody, Ted would always stand between them.

A lump filled her throat, but she refused to cry. She'd cried too many tears already. Now she needed to be practical and think of where her brother could be holed up.

Flipping on the radio, she turned the knob until the static cleared and the weather report came on. The sky looked clear, but this time of year storms blew in without warning.

Her thoughts turned again to that stormy night so long ago. She saw the angry waves pounding the side of her father's cabin cruiser. The rain, the wind…

The marina.

Why hadn't she thought of it earlier?

Pushing down on the accelerator, she headed south and then west, toward Big Island Lake where her father kept his boats.

She shivered. Surely Ted wouldn't take *The Upton Queen* or *The Princess* out onto the water. Not when he was so mixed-up with the turmoil bubbling around him.

"Oh, please, God, keep him safe."

Surprised by calling on the Lord again this evening, she turned on her high beams and raced along the back roads. Brody followed behind her.

Her phone rang, but before she could answer, it went to voice mail. The call was probably from Brody, wondering where they were headed.

A second call came in.

She raised the cell to her ear. "Brody?"

"Ah, no, Steph. It's Paul."

The soldier's voice sounded thick with alcohol.

"I called a minute ago and left a voice mail. Then I thought I'd try you a second time. I just got your message about the appointment with the shrink tomorrow."

"It's at two in the afternoon, Paul. Actually, she's a social worker, not a psychiatrist. But she's good at what she does and she wants to help."

"I don't want help, Steph. You've got it all wrong. I'm not having any problems."

"Paul, you've been drinking. Where are you?"

"I'm home."

"Go to bed and get some rest. We'll talk in the morning. You haven't seen Ted, have you?"

"He wants to be alone. Ted told me he doesn't need you."

"Maybe not, but I need him."

Hopefully, in the morning, once Paul had slept off the effects of his night of drinking, he'd realize counseling would be helpful.

Her mother always said things happened for a reason. Maybe it was good that Ted had run away this evening; otherwise, he might have been drinking with Paul.

As she neared the marina, a bell tolled in the night, the bell on her father's boat. She parked and stepped to the pavement as Brody pulled to a stop beside her.

"Stay here. Ted's by the water. I don't want him any more upset than he already is."

"He could have a gun, Stephanie."

She shook her head, tired of Brody's incessant attempts to make Ted into a killer. "He's my brother. Let me talk to him alone."

"I'll be waiting at the entrance to the dock."

"I don't need your help, Brody."

"I'm not leaving you."

"That's your choice, but don't interfere."

She stomped off, angry that he was so intent on staying put and yet grateful he was there. Her father had scoffed any time she had been afraid. Having someone who put her safety first was a good thing. Just as long as Ted didn't see Brody as a threat.

She hurried along the wooden ramp. Ted stood beside the cabin cruiser and stared into the water. His right hand was wrapped around the rope attached to the bell. Every few seconds, he yanked on the cord.

"Ted."

Hearing her voice, he turned. "How'd you find me?"

She eased forward. "I went everyplace else first. The marina was the only place left to look. I should have known you'd be here. That day on the lake, I…I was mad at you."

"You forbade me to go out on the water. I told you I was spending the day at Paul's house. Only that was a lie."

She took a step closer. "I was proud of you for not going with the other kids. I baked a cake for you so we could celebrate your good decision."

He glanced back at the water. "I didn't think you'd find out, and I didn't care if you did."

"You were angry about our mother's death. It wasn't your fault, Ted."

"I wanted you home with me."

"Mom asked me to continue my studies."

"She always thought of your needs instead of her own."

"College was important to her, Ted. She had to drop out of school when her own mother died. She didn't want the same thing to happen to me." Holding out her hand, she beckoned him forward. "Let's go home."

He shook his head. "You don't want me there."

"That's not true. I changed the alarm because someone came into the house a few nights ago. They left a note that said I never should have come back to

Freemont. I wanted to ensure that person wouldn't get inside again."

"Did you think I left the note?"

She shook her head. "I knew it wasn't you."

He glanced up at the top of the marina where Brody stood watching them.

Ted pointed. "He thought I hurt Joshua. He probably thought I'd left the note."

"I told him you didn't, Ted." She glanced at Brody. "He believed me."

Ted sighed. "Can I stay at the house tonight?"

"Of course." Once again, she held out her hand.

He dropped the cord on the bell and shuffled toward her, his head hung and shoulders slumped.

Her heart broke for him and for the struggle he was undergoing internally, a struggle that needed to be healed. He had opened up tonight. Hopefully, it was a good start that would continue in the days ahead. If only he trusted her enough to know that she wouldn't let him down again.

Together they walked to where Brody stood.

"We're going home," she told him.

"Major Jenkins expects Ted back at the WTB."

"Call Jenkins, Brody." Her voice was firm. "Tell him he'll be there in the morning."

She helped Ted into the car and turned to find Brody staring at her, the frustration in his eyes making it clear he didn't approve of her decision.

"I won't leave him, Brody. A door has opened just a crack. Maybe it can open even more tonight."

"It's not safe for you to be alone with him, Stephanie."

"You're thinking of the past and not the present. I told you before. I'm not Lisa."

He clamped down on his jaw. "I'm well aware of who you are. Stubborn and headstrong." He shook his head and sighed. "But you're also determined to help your brother, and I admire you for that. Let me stay at the house. If anything happens, I'll be there."

She shook her head. "I need to do this alone."

Stephanie slipped into the driver's seat, not knowing what would happen during the night. She had this one chance with Ted, and she wouldn't do anything to ruin that fragile beginning to a new relationship.

As she pulled onto the main road, she looked into her rearview mirror. Brody was standing under one of the lights in the marina parking lot. He didn't understand, because he was still trying to make up for what had happened to his girlfriend. That was his personal struggle.

Just as she had hers.

Life wasn't easy. No one said it would be, and sometimes she felt totally alone. But tonight she had Ted beside her.

Coming back to Freemont may have been the right decision after all, if she and Ted could heal their relationship.

And Brody? Would he ever be able to forget what had happened? If he could move beyond the past, there might be hope for them. But right now, he was too focused on being a special agent instead of a man who cared about the future.

* * *

Heavyhearted, Brody stood at the entrance to the marina. Stephanie had made her choice and refused to listen to his concerns about her safety.

Once her taillights disappeared from sight, he let out a deep sigh and turned to look at the Upton cabin cruiser. It was state-of-the-art and a boater's dream, yet Stephanie wanted nothing to do with the luxury craft.

He pulled out his phone, clicked on the photo he had saved from the Freemont paper and watched it unfold across his screen.

A water-drenched Stephanie stood on the deck of the cabin cruiser, a blanket hung around her shoulders. Her eyes were wide, and a look of shock and disbelief wrapped around her face.

Her brother was also onboard. Nikki huddled next to him. Paul and Joshua were sitting, shoulders slumped, while EMTs worked on a woman who appeared to be Cindy.

Stephanie had taken her father's larger craft to the island that day. The painful memories probably kept her from boarding the cabin cruiser again.

Brody could relate. He hadn't sketched since Lisa's death.

His phone rang.

"Goodman."

"It's Nikki. I'm worried about Ted. He's not answering his cell. Stephanie's phone goes to voice mail, too."

"They're together and heading back to their house."

"I'm so glad."

Brody wished he shared her enthusiasm. "Your car's parked at the marina, Nikki. Can someone give you a ride in the morning?"

"I'll call Paul."

On his way back to post, Brody phoned Major Jenkins. "Private Upton's with his sister. He plans to stay at home tonight. Stephanie will drive him back to the WTB in the morning."

"You sound worried."

"I told Stephanie she was putting herself in danger. She refuses to see beyond the fact that he's her brother."

"Being with his sister might do Ted good."

Brody wasn't as optimistic as the major. When he disconnected, he contacted Don Palmer at home. "Sorry to bother you, Chief, but I need a favor. Any chance you could increase surveillance again tonight in the Country Club Estates, specifically the Upton home?"

"Did something else happen?"

"Only that Stephanie and her brother are together, trying to reconcile."

"But you're worried?"

"I just want her to be safe."

The chief sighed. "Okay, I'll increase the patrols and instruct my officers to keep their eyes and ears open."

"I owe you, sir."

"Help me wrap up this investigation, and we'll call it even."

Once back on post, Brody headed to the hospital and the ICU, relieved that Joshua was still holding on.

Brody approached the soldier's bedside.

Joshua had sacrificed his own well-being for his country and had come home as a double amputee. Adversity hadn't dampened his enthusiasm for life, from what Major Jenkins had said. But to have the attack happen when he was trying to make a future for himself...

"Why, Lord?" Brody couldn't understand how a loving God decided who would live and who would die.

Lisa. Hayden.

Those two deaths had changed Brody and Stephanie's lives. Both of them were still too caught up in the past.

Would he ever be able to get over what had happened? What about Stephanie? Would she ever be able to move beyond Hayden's death?

No matter how much Brody wished things would be different, he and Stephanie didn't have a chance. Their paths would soon part and stay apart no matter how much he wished things would be different.

SEVENTEEN

Stephanie and Ted talked until his eyes grew heavy, and she knew he needed sleep. After he headed to his room, she retrieved the messages from her cell phone. Nikki had called a number of times to check on Ted.

The concern she heard in the girl's voice warmed her heart. Nikki seemed to genuinely care about Ted's well-being. A refreshing change from the way Brody regarded her brother.

The last voice mail from Nikki was more ominous.

"I've been trying to get Paul on his cell and home landline, but he fails to answer. I know he was upset about Josh and wanted to be alone tonight. It's not like Paul to ignore my calls. I'm worried, Stephanie. Could you check on him?"

Glancing at her watch, Stephanie groaned. Almost eleven-thirty. Too late to be traipsing around the neighborhood. Surely by now, he'd be sleeping off the effects of the alcohol and probably wouldn't respond, even if she pounded on his front door.

Still, he was a good kid and Ted's friend. If anything

happened, she'd feel responsible, and she didn't need more guilt piled on her already-overloaded shoulders.

Quickly, she wrote a note for Ted and left it on the kitchen counter, not far from where she'd found the typed message and marked photograph of the old high school gang.

No need to think of the past, she reminded herself. She and Ted were in a better place. Grabbing her purse, she quietly left the house and climbed into the Cadillac parked at the curb.

Within a few minutes, she pulled in front of the Massey home. Just as earlier this evening, the front porch was dark, but a light in the rear cast the backyard in shadows. Perhaps Paul was on the deck. Hopefully, he wasn't still drowning his sorrows.

She shivered, realizing the significance of the expression, especially since the Masseys had a pool and hot tub. Cross one bridge at a time, her mother used to say.

Determined to find Paul, hopefully groggy with sleep, and then hurry back to her own house, Stephanie climbed the steps to the front porch. She rang the bell three times and then pounded her hand against the heavy oak.

When he failed to respond, she rounded the house and called Paul's name as she approached the backyard. Light from the overhead deck played over the pool. Her stomach tightened thinking of what she could find. If only she had brought her phone. Knowing she could call for help would have bolstered her courage. Instead, she had inadvertently left it on the counter at home. As much as she didn't want to be prowling around Paul's house, she needed to be certain he was okay.

Working to ignore the nervous tingle that played along her spine, she neared the wrought-iron fence surrounding the pool and peered into the water, seeing nothing except dark shadows.

Flicking her gaze over the patio area, she spied the hot tub in the far corner. The plastic top sat askew. Strange to have it half on, half off, especially in the middle of the summer.

A beach towel sat neatly folded on a nearby lounge chair. Her pulse kicked up a notch. She swallowed, her throat dry, her palms suddenly moist. She wiped them over her skirt, knowing she had no recourse except to enter the fenced enclosure.

The gate creaked as it swung open. A gust of hot, humid air rustled through the trees and caught her hair. She tugged the loose strands out of her face and blinked, willing her eyes to adjust to the darkened area under the deck where the plastic lid held her focus.

Her heart thumped a warning as she neared.

"Paul?"

She glanced again at the beach towel, then lowered her gaze to where something lay under the corner of the chaise.

An empty vodka bottle.

Her breath hitched and a roar filled her ears.

Bending down, she grabbed the plastic lip of the hot-tub cover, raised the lid and peered into the shallow pool.

Her heart stopped. The patio swirled around her as her knees buckled.

She screamed at seeing Paul Massey's eyes staring at her from under the water.

"Thanks for notifying me," Brody said to the Freemont police chief. Three patrols cars sat in front of the Massey home, their lights flickering through the night. Officers milled about on the front lawn while the crime-scene team worked in the patio area.

"I need to thank you for requesting extra surveillance," the chief said. "One of my men happened by just as Ms. Upton ran screaming from the backyard."

Brody glanced at the patrol car where Stephanie sat hunched over in the backseat.

"At this point everything appears fairly cut-and-dried," Palmer continued. "Paul left a suicide note and mentioned wanting to ease Joshua Webb's misery." The chief shook his head. "Luckily, he wasn't successful on that count."

The chief filled Brody in on what had happened and then pointed to the squad car. "If you want to talk to Ms. Upton, I'm ready to send her home. She's been very cooperative."

Stephanie glanced up as Brody approached. Her face was noticeably pale and drawn. Fatigue added to the worry he saw on her furrowed brow and tight lips.

"You doing okay?" he asked, hoping she heard concern and understanding in his voice.

"Not really."

"I'm sorry you had to find him."

Tears filled her eyes. "Nikki called me. She was worried something might be wrong. I never…" She swallowed. "I never thought…"

"I'll drive you home."

She handed Brody the keys to her father's car. He wrapped his arm around her shoulders and ushered her forward, out of the glare of the police lights.

She was silent on the way to the house.

"May I come in?" he asked as they climbed the stairs to her front porch. "We need to talk."

She shook her head. "Not tonight. I…I have to get some sleep."

"You shouldn't be alone, Stephanie."

"Ted's still here. I'll be okay."

He unlocked the door, and she hesitated before stepping inside. "It's over, isn't it?"

"You mean about Josh?"

"And Ted. Chief Palmer said Paul left a note. You can't blame my brother anymore."

Brody wished he could assure Stephanie, but while Ted was no longer a suspect in Joshua's attack, he had showed too much antagonism for Brody to give him a total pass now. Only time would tell.

Which Stephanie wouldn't want to hear.

She must have suspected the reason for his hesitation because, with a heavy sigh, she hurried into the house and closed the door behind her. The dead bolt clicked into place.

"Good night, Stephanie."

He double-timed back to the Massey home. He wanted to see the crime scene for himself. Too many questions needed to be answered, but his thoughts continued to revolve around Stephanie and how he wished things could be different.

As much as Brody didn't want to look back, he also didn't want to think about tomorrow and the day after that and the day following if it meant he wouldn't have Stephanie.

Stephanie woke the next morning to someone pounding on her door. She glanced at the clock. Six a.m.

Wrapping her robe around her waist, she hurried along the front hallway, hoping the knocking wouldn't awaken her brother.

She peered out the front window, somewhat relieved when she recognized the car in the driveway.

Pulling open the door, she squared her shoulders.

"Brody, why in the world are you pounding on my door at this hour?"

"I need to talk to Ted."

She groaned. "Haven't we been down this path before?"

"He's still here, isn't he, Stephanie?"

"Yes, but he's sleeping."

"The note Paul supposedly left had the same flawed *o.* Just like the note in your kitchen."

"Paul wrote the warning?"

"I checked the printers in his house. The letters weren't smeared."

"Which means what?"

"Which means the suicide note may have been written by someone else. Someone who planned to do Paul harm. That's why I need to bring Ted in for questioning."

The air sucked from her lungs. She took a step back. Surely Brody didn't suspect Ted. "Did the medical examiner determine when Paul died?"

"The M.E. provided an estimate. Sometime between nine and midnight."

"That rules out Ted," she said.

"How can you be so certain?"

"My brother and I were together from ten o'clock on. You were at the marina with us."

"He could have killed him earlier."

"Impossible. Paul called me at nine-fifty. He'd been drinking. I pulled into the marina and saw Ted minutes later."

"Show me your phone."

Hurt that he didn't believe her, she steeled her jaw. Brody was determined to find Ted at fault no matter what evidence she provided.

Retrieving her cell, she showed Brody the call log. "Do you see the time the call came in? Nine-fifty, which was when I was approaching the marina. No other cars passed me en route, and Ted was at the marina by the time I arrived. I told the chief last night."

She pointed to the phone. "Access voice mail and you'll hear the message Paul left initially. He sounded drunk and said he was going to bed. I thought he needed to sleep off his binge. In hindsight, I should have notified someone. When Nikki phoned and told me he hadn't responded to her calls, I decided to check on him."

"You could have phoned me." Brody worked the prompts and lifted her cell to his ear. Once Paul's message had completed playing, he lowered the phone.

"The Freemont police will need to listen to the message and check the time frame. They also need to talk to Ted."

She stared at Brody, unable to comprehend how he could continue to think Ted was at fault.

Her brother's bedroom door opened. "Is something wrong?"

Brody stepped inside. "You need to come with me to police headquarters, Private Upton."

"You called him?" Ted looked from Brody to Stephanie. "All of this was so you could set me up."

The advances they had made last night collapsed in that one moment. Her relationship with her brother had hit rock bottom.

Would she ever be able to explain the truth about what had happened?

Would Ted believe her?

Only if Brody was out of her life.

EIGHTEEN

The next three days were rainy and overcast, which fit Brody's mood. Paul's voice mail to Stephanie and her assurance to the Freemont police that she had found her brother at the marina shortly after the message had been sent confirmed Ted's innocence.

Paul had told a number of people in town that Joshua didn't want to live as an amputee. The chief of police was convinced Paul had planned a mercy killing, which Stephanie had prevented by finding Joshua in the nick of time. When Paul's plan failed, he had become despondent and had taken his own life.

The case was wrapped up, at least as far as the Freemont police were concerned. Brody had his doubts. Mainly because of the so-called suicide note Paul had left with the blurred print.

Plus, he had died in his parents' hot tub. An empty bottle of vodka had been found nearby. The police believed he'd gotten drunk, lost consciousness and drowned. All of which could indicate an accidental death, if not for the note.

Brody rubbed his temples and ignored the half-filled

cup of coffee on his desk. He'd had too much caffeine over the past three days.

Too much caffeine and not enough sleep.

Every night, thoughts of Stephanie kept him pacing the floor in his BOQ.

He checked his watch and headed to Chief Wilson's office. "Sir, I'll be at the Main Post Chapel for Private Paul Massey's funeral. I've requested two men from the military police to join me there. Jamison said he'd be there, as well."

"You're still not convinced the death was a suicide?"

"It's a gut feeling, sir, but drowning in a hot tub doesn't seem the way a soldier would take his own life. A bullet hole to the head would be more logical in my opinion."

The chief rubbed his chin. "The stats would prove you right. But you need evidence to back up your hunch."

If only Brody could find the printer with the blurred vowel.

"What about Joshua Webb's condition?" the chief asked.

"Still guarded. He's been on antibiotic therapy to counter the infection and was improving. Then the bacteria that caused the infection became resistant to the medication. The doc's trying another combination of antimicrobials, but he's not optimistic."

"Have you talked to the AW2 advocate?"

"Not since her brother was questioned by the Freemont police."

"PFC Upton will attend the funeral?"

"I believe so."

"Watch him."

"Yes, sir."

The heavy chords of the organ filled the sanctuary when Brody entered the Main Post Chapel. A steady flow of mourners streamed into the pews, many in uniform. Even more were civilians, friends of the family, no doubt, from Freemont.

Brody stood in the rear and searched for Stephanie. Hearing the clip of high heels, he turned as she entered the church.

Their eyes locked for half a heartbeat before she glanced away and walked toward the front of the church. Nikki followed her into a pew and scooted over to make room for Cindy.

Brody clamped down on his jaw, steeling himself to her rebuff. Deep down, he had hoped time would temper her feelings toward him.

As much as he wished things could have been different, Brody wouldn't have changed the way he had handled the situation. He still wasn't sure Ted was completely stable.

His phone vibrated. Stepping outside, he raised the cell to his ear.

Instead of a greeting, the Freemont chief of police quickly explained the reason for his call. "The toxicology report came back on Paul Massey."

Brody smiled. "You must have friends in high places."

The chief laughed. "I told them the case involved U.S. Army heroes and needed to be handled stat."

"As quickly as you got the results back, they must have listened. Did they find anything?"

"Clonazepam. It's in the benzodiazepine family of drugs."

"Usually prescribed for panic attacks."

"That's right. As well as seizures. Law enforcement in Atlanta is keeping a sharp eye on the drug because of its street use."

"As a date-rape drug." Brody was well aware of clonazepam's side effects.

"Exactly. Which may shoot my suicide theory out of the water."

"Unless Paul was having panic attacks. I'll contact the head of the hospital at his last duty station and request a copy of his medical records. You'll question the local docs to find out whether he got a prescription around here?"

"I've already got two officers doing exactly that. They're also contacting the area pharmacies. I'll notify you if I hear anything."

Brody disconnected and watched the hearse pull to a stop in front of the chapel. Six pallbearers spilled from the narthex. Ted Upton walked next to Keith Allen.

Dressed in his military uniform, Ted looked strong and stoic, but the twitch in his cheek and the downward turn to his shoulders spoke volumes about how he really felt.

Paul Massey's parents—an older couple with drawn faces—stood nearby. The woman leaned into the man for support and dabbed a tissue at the corners of her eyes.

As the chaplain greeted the family, Brody slipped past them and reentered the sanctuary. Stephanie glanced back as if sensing his return.

Trying to ignore her gaze, he nodded to the two military policemen standing in the rear. Earlier, he had briefed them about watching the crowd gathered at the funeral and cemetery and to alert him to anything that seemed suspect. Jamison Steele was on-site, as well.

The deep, resonating sounds of the organ filled the church. The congregation stood and began to sing. The pallbearers proceeded up the middle aisle, carrying the casket. Ted glanced at Brody as he passed. The private's face was pale and drawn.

The family followed and filed into the front pew on the left. The pallbearers entered the pew directly opposite. At the conclusion of the hymn, the chaplain approached the pulpit and opened the service with prayer.

Brody bowed his head, thinking back to Lisa's funeral. The minister that day had preached words of consolation, but all Brody could remember was his own despair.

Fisting his hands, he refused to dwell on the past and instead flicked his gaze around the sanctuary, knowing someone in the congregation could have attacked Joshua and staged Paul's death to look like a suicide.

Was clonazepam the missing link in this twisted chain of events? Or was there something else Brody wasn't seeing?

Once again, he visualized the filled bathtub in Josh's home. Had the attacker planned to drown Joshua?

Stephanie's arrival could have forced the perpetrator to flee before he had time to submerge Josh in the water.

Stored on his phone, the newspaper photo of the teens huddled on the Upton boat flashed through his mind. What if one of them was avenging Hayden's death?

His gaze settled on Nikki. She and Hayden had gone to prom together. Had she fallen for the town's shining star and lashed out when the returning soldiers came back to Freemont, angry at those who had lived when the boy she loved had died?

Nikki knew the schedule at the bakery and had even voiced concern that Ted could have inherited his mother's allergy. Easy enough for her to send Stephanie cookies, knowing she was allergic.

But would she have left the note and bull's-eye in the house? She would have needed a key to get inside, which Ted could have provided, along with the code for the security alarm.

Were Nikki and Ted working together? Or was Ted guilty and acting alone, just as Brody had suspected all along?

Was he avenging Hayden's death, or had something happened that day on the lake that Ted, in an emotional state brought on by PTSD, wanted to cover up by killing the other guys involved?

"We know the past always has bearing on our lives." The chaplain's voice filled the church. "Our relationship with the Lord forms who we are and how we react in situations. Paul was a fine son and a good friend to everyone who knew him. He was also a military hero who put his country first."

Brody watched Ted's response. He sat with his arms folded across his chest and appeared to be grieving. As Brody knew too well, looks could be deceiving.

"Although we will never know exactly what happened the night Paul died," the chaplain continued, "we do know death is not the end but the beginning of new life lived with the Lord. The pain of the present world is over for Paul. He has journeyed home, which should bring comfort and peace."

Brody signaled to the military policemen and then Jamison that he was leaving. As he stepped into the humid afternoon, the minister's words replayed in his mind. Would he ever be able to look beyond the horrific circumstances of Lisa's death?

If only he could believe in a loving and compassionate God, then perhaps he would see hope for the future and have some sense of peace about the past.

He'd been given a second chance with Stephanie, but that relationship had failed, and now, just as before, he was on his own.

Stephanie needed someone he could never be.

The realization tore at him and made Brody want to pound his fist into a wall.

To distance himself from the pain, he pulled his cell from his pocket and called Chief Wilson. "Sir, I need to make a stop on post. Then I'll head to Freemont to talk to the chief of police. I feel there's an area of the investigation we haven't explored."

"Take as much time as you need."

The chief's response was what Brody had hoped to hear. He phoned Don Palmer and told him his latest idea. "I'll stop at the Post Exchange and check their computer printers. I suggest you do the same at the bakery in town."

"You think Nikki's involved?"

"Actually, I still think Ted's our most likely suspect. But he and Nikki are friends. I want to ensure she didn't help him out. You might question Nikki's sister. See if anyone in the family takes clonazepam."

"What about Ted?"

"I talked to the medical-care team at the Warrior Transitional Battalion. He's on medication, but not that particular drug."

"What about his sister? Could she be taking it?"

Brody didn't appreciate the inference. "Let's put that on hold for now until we learn about Nikki and Ted's involvement."

By the time he arrived at police headquarters, Brody was less than optimistic. None of the PX printers produced the flawed letters. The chief didn't find anything at the bakery, either, and no one in Nikki's family was under medical care.

According to the sister, Nikki didn't have a computer or printer and relied on her smart phone and the library in town when she needed the internet. The chief sent one of his men to check the library printers, but he soon returned empty-handed.

By evening, Brody felt discouraged. He and the chief continued to hash over the information they had for a few more hours, until finally, at eight o'clock, Brody knew it was time to go home.

He left police headquarters eager to watch Braves baseball and focus on his favorite team instead of the case, but when he slid behind the wheel, he spied Keith's folder with the information about the Wounded Warrior picnic. Information Stephanie needed. Brody smiled. Information that would provide a reason for him to stop by her house this evening.

He shook his head. Stephanie didn't want to see him, he felt sure, and he was too tired to dance around the conflict that stood between them. Especially when he planned to, once again, haul Ted in for questioning in the next day or two.

Go home and stop thinking about Stephanie, his voice of reason cautioned.

The truth was, he couldn't get her out of his thoughts. Even more troubling, he couldn't get her out of his heart.

NINETEEN

"Don't think about him," Stephanie told herself as she puttered around the house, struggling to keep her mind on anything except Brody. She had looked for him after the interment, but he was nowhere to be found.

What would she have said if he had found him? Perhaps they would have chatted about inconsequential topics that skirted the real issue that was lodged between them.

If only Brody would hang up his badge and his gun at times and be a friend instead of a special agent. At one point, she had hoped their friendship would blossom into something more long lasting. Now she doubted there was anything to salvage.

Brody seemed antagonistic, if not confrontational, toward her brother. She couldn't invite into her life someone who harbored ill feelings toward Ted, especially when she and her brother were beginning to find common ground.

Ted had come back to the house briefly with Nikki after the funeral. Keith and Cindy had stopped by, as well. Everyone wanted to reminisce about Paul and old times. Before the day at the lake. Before the boys had enlisted.

Now that they had left, Stephanie needed fresh air to clear her mind. She poured a second glass of iced tea from the pitcher in the refrigerator that she had served earlier and took a long, cool sip before she carried the glass onto the patio. The group had been nice enough to help clean up the kitchen and put away the snacks before they left, which Stephanie appreciated.

She settled into one of the chairs by the pool. A light breeze tugged at her hair and provided a reprieve from the heat.

Her phone chirped. She smiled when she saw Ted's name on her call screen.

"Hey, Steph." He sounded good. "I'm back at the barracks for the night, and my squad leader stopped by to make sure I was doing okay. He said to alert him if I have any problems."

"I'm glad, Ted. Don't hesitate to ask for help if you can't sleep or are troubled by dreams."

"Joshua's condition hasn't improved." Ted hesitated for a long moment. "The sergeant suggested I pray for him."

Which Nikki had mentioned. "That sounds like a good idea."

"Would you pray, too?"

She had closed God out of her life, but maybe it was time to make a change. "Yes, I'll pray."

She disconnected, feeling a warm sense of relief well up inside her. Her troubled relationship with her brother was starting to improve. Reaching once again for the glass of tea, her hand trembled.

Too much caffeine, perhaps, or too little sleep.

She hadn't gotten a good night's rest since she'd found Joshua on his bathroom floor. The sergeant was right. The injured soldier needed prayers. So did Ted.

Lord, help both guys heal.

She should go back inside, but her eyes were heavy. Totally relaxed, she struggled to remain awake. Her chin dropped to her chest.

A sound interrupted her sleep.

Startled, she tried to turn toward the shuffling footsteps and raised voice, but her body wouldn't respond to her promptings. Unable to decipher the words that were blurred with rage, she flicked her gaze over her shoulder but saw only darkness.

A forceful weight slammed into her from behind. With a gasp, she fell onto the patio. Her head hit the concrete. Pain shot through her skull.

She groaned and clawed at the rough surface, trying to escape from the voice that railed through her.

Someone kicked her. Pain ricocheted through her lower back.

"No," she moaned.

Cowering, she huddled in a protective ball and tried to fend off strikes that came one after another.

Rough hands grabbed her arms and half lifted, half dragged her across the patio toward the pool. She thrashed against their hold, unable to break free.

With a forceful heave, she was shoved into the shimmering water. Gulping air, she tried to stay afloat, but her limbs hung heavy, like deadweight.

She swallowed a mouthful of water and coughed. Unable to remain buoyant, she slipped beneath the surface.

Gravity pulled her downward into the deep abyss. She couldn't breathe.

Garbled though it was through the water, she heard laughter, maniacal laughter that intensified her fear.

Her lungs burned. She tried to push off from the bottom and realized too late the horrible reality that she would drown, just like Hayden.

Another sound. The clang of a bell ringing over and over again.

If only someone would save her.

Brody?

She had closed him out of her life. He would never find her. At least, not in time.

TWENTY

Pulling to the curb outside the Upton home, Brody grabbed his phone and the file folder before he stepped to the sidewalk. He had planned to go home to Fort Rickman, but an overwhelming need to see Stephanie forced him to drive instead to the Country Club Estates.

The stillness of the night was shattered by the knell of the maritime bell. His blood chilled. Forgoing the front door, he raced around the house to the patio.

A shadowed form darted into the thick wooded area at the back of the property. Brody turned his gaze to the patio. A wrought-iron chair lay overturned. The pool gate hung open.

His breath hitched. Fear jammed his throat.

He ran to the water's edge and dropped the folder and cell to the concrete. His heart exploded when he glanced into the pool.

"Stephanie."

Diving into the water, he was oblivious to everything except her limp body lying on the bottom of the pool.

He pulled her into his arms and kicked violently, propelling both of them to the surface. With three strong strokes, he carried her to the edge of the pool and lifted her onto the deck. Kneeling next to her, he pushed down on her sternum with rapid thrusts.

How long had she been submerged? If only she would respond.

"God, help me," he pleaded, knowing he didn't deserve a response from the Lord. But Stephanie did. "Please, Lord."

She coughed and sputtered.

"Open your eyes, honey. It's Brody. You're going to be all right."

He swallowed hard, trying to keep his emotions in check. Her eyes fluttered open. "I'm here, honey. You're going to be okay."

"Br…Brody?" Her voice was only a ragged whisper.

He nodded. "You were at the bottom of the pool. Who did it, Stephanie? Was it Ted?"

She grimaced.

"Or Nikki?"

She shook her head and tried to sit up, but she didn't have the strength.

Brody reached for his cell phone, lying nearby, and called the Freemont chief of police. Quickly, Brody filled him in on what had happened.

"Stephanie's responsive, but I want to know for certain she's okay. Send an ambulance and medical personnel."

The chief assured him the EMTs would arrive

shortly, and that he, along with two other police officers, were on their way.

A number of sheets of paper had spilled from the file folder and lay scattered on the concrete. Brody lifted one of the pages and stared at the print.

The letter *o* had the same flawed type as the warning message left on Stephanie's counter and the suicide note found near the hot tub at Paul Massey's house.

Brody shook his head in amazement. They finally had the evidence they needed. "We've got our killer," he told the chief. "You'll never believe who it is."

"Keith Allen?"

Stephanie sat in her living room and sipped a cup of tea. She had been in the emergency room for more hours than she wanted to count. A cherry-flavored drink that contained charcoal rid the remaining drugs from her system. Although the doctor had wanted to keep her overnight for observation, she had insisted on going home. The lab had tested the iced-tea pitcher and found a high level of clonazepam in the liquid that Keith must have added before leaving her house.

Brody paced back and forth across the living room, visibly agitated by her close call.

"I should have been with you," he berated himself.

"You saved me, Brody, for which I'm grateful. Now stop pacing and try to relax. Keith has been arrested and the danger has passed."

She shook her head, trying to get a handle on everything that had occurred. "But why would Keith kill Paul and attack Joshua? It doesn't make sense."

"Not to us, but to someone vindictive about his brother's death it might seem logical. Keith was probably angry because Hayden had died while Paul and Joshua survived."

"If that were the case, wouldn't Keith be equally hostile toward Ted?"

Brody shrugged. "Maybe he had listed the guys in alphabetical order. Joshua. Paul. Ted would have been next."

Stephanie shuddered, thinking of what could have been.

Footsteps sounded on the porch. A key turned the lock. She glanced toward the front door.

Ted and Nikki stepped inside and hurried to the couch where Stephanie sat. Nikki hugged her and Ted squeezed her hand. "Glad you're okay, sis."

At least they were making progress.

She glanced at Nikki. "Are you sure spending the night won't put you out?"

"Of course not. You shouldn't be alone. I don't have to go to work until noon tomorrow."

"And I plan to be at my desk much earlier than that," Stephanie assured her.

"Ted's taking my car back to the barracks tonight," Nikki said. "He'll pick me up tomorrow."

Ted shook his head as if dumbfounded by what had happened. "I still can't believe Keith attacked you and killed Paul."

"He may have felt overwhelmed with guilt for his brother's death. I always thought Keith had provided the alcohol that day on the lake." Stephanie kept her eyes trained on Ted. He refused to hold her gaze.

"Hayden knew where the bottles had been hidden," Nikki said. "I thought he had stolen them from Keith and stashed them on the island. Isn't that what you thought, Ted?"

He shrugged. "Sounds right to me."

"Did you know there would be alcohol that day, Ted?"

"I thought it was a just a picnic."

But he had consumed the whiskey, just as the other kids had. Temptation was often too hard to resist.

She looked at Brody. He hadn't wanted her to be alone, but he'd voiced opposition to Nikki staying overnight. With Keith behind bars, Stephanie had assured him she would be fine.

His first question after he had saved her life was whether she had seen her attacker. His next question had torn her heart in two. *"Was it Ted?"*

The CID agent would always think Ted was at fault. Then he had mentioned Nikki.

As much as she hated to admit the truth, she and Brody didn't have a future together, not when he continued to look for fault in her brother.

Ted had made mistakes in his past, but he was trying to be a better man and find his way in life. Stephanie was confident that with counseling Ted would heal, but he had to be surrounded by people who believed in him.

Brody would cause more harm than good. No matter how much she cared about the handsome CID agent, she couldn't open her heart to someone so opposed to her brother. Especially now, when her relationship with Ted was starting to mend.

TWENTY-ONE

The sky was overcast on Saturday. The weatherman predicted showers, but not until evening, long after the Wounded Warrior picnic.

Brody called the chief of police as he drove to the marina. "Any chance the judge will set bail in the Allen case?"

"Not until Monday. We've got Keith locked up at least for the weekend, although he insists he's not guilty."

"Did you mention the printer in his office?"

"And the clonazepam we found in his desk drawer. Keith refilled the prescription last week, yet half the pills were gone. He only takes them when he feels a panic attack coming on. Or so he says."

"Evidently he's panicked a lot recently," Brody said.

"Exactly."

"He stopped by Stephanie's house after the funeral. That's when he must have drugged the pitcher of iced tea."

"He claims he's been framed," Palmer said. "He even asked that his arrest be kept from his mother. I talked to the administrator of the nursing home. He passed the message on to the staff. At this point, that's all we can do." The cop sighed. "I feel for his mom. Tough to lose one son to death and another through crime."

"If the jury finds him guilty." Brody thought about Ted. Had he been wrong about the soldier all along? "Keith doesn't strike me as a killer."

"You still suspect Ted Upton?"

Brody let out a pent up breath. "I'm trying to determine how he fits into the picture. There's something he's not telling me."

"And his sister?"

"She believes her brother isn't at fault."

"We all need someone like that on our side," the chief said.

Brody had to agree, but Stephanie had made it perfectly clear she wanted nothing to do with him once the picnic was over. He'd brought it on himself with his constant concern for her safety.

As much as he needed to distance himself from Stephanie, she continued to be part of his life. Last night, he had dreamed of holding her in his arms and kissing her sweet lips.

Maybe he'd put in for temporary duty. Wilson needed someone to fill a slot in D.C. Getting away from Fort Rickman might be a good thing, at least until he could get a handle on where his life was headed—a life without Stephanie.

The marina appeared in the distance. Brody pulled into the parking lot and walked to where a number of military personnel were loading picnic items onto *The Princess*. A larger military craft was already on the lake, heading to the island, no doubt filled with the bulk of the supplies. Cadre from the Warrior Transitional Battalion were helping out and working side by side with volunteers from town.

Despite Keith's arrest, it looked as if the local merchants were determined to make the event a success for the soldiers.

Hefting a box from the dock, Brody placed it on Stephanie's boat. A gust of wind tugged at her hair. She pulled it back and smiled.

"Thanks."

"The cloud cover might keep the temperature down today," he offered as a greeting.

Her smile faded. "I talked to the meteorologist on post. He said the weather should be clear and bright." She glanced skyward. "He failed to mention the overcast sky and stiff breeze."

"What time is the unit scheduled to arrive?"

"Soon. Major Jenkins authorized a bus to transport the soldiers. A number of local folks will boat them over to the island."

"What about Ted?"

Stephanie averted her gaze. "He's arriving with the unit. Nikki is already on the island. She started cooking early this morning. Cindy's helping with the games. From her connections at the garage, she got a lot of the local townsfolk to help."

"Has anyone mentioned Keith?"

"Only that they don't think he's a killer."

"Did they provide the name of a more likely suspect?"

She shook her head. "Not that I heard. Although I know you have your suspicions."

"I don't think Ted harmed Paul or Joshua, Stephanie."

She turned with wide eyes to gaze up at him. "Really?"

"I was wrong, and I'm sorry. But I still worry about his stability and will continue to be concerned until the counselors tell me that he's worked through what happened in Afghanistan."

She shook her head. "You never change, do you, Brody?"

"If you mean I can never stop being a cop, you're probably right. I always imagine worst-case scenarios so I'm not surprised when bad things happen. Plus, I what-if each situation."

"You worst-cased my relationship with my brother because of your own past. I told you we're different, but you're unable to accept anything I say about Ted."

"Maybe Ted isn't the problem."

She inhaled sharply. "What's that mean?"

"You didn't tell me everything about that day on the lake and what happened between you and your brother."

Before she could reply, the bus filled with soldiers pulled into the parking lot. They disembarked with shouts of revelry and laughter and quickly filed onto the various boats waiting to transport them.

"I'll see you on the island," Brody told Stephanie.

He waited until her brother boarded one of the boats and then took a seat near him. If Ted couldn't handle returning to the island, Brody would be close by to keep things from getting out of hand.

Once they docked, Brody helped unload the supplies. He carried the food items to the kitchen where Nikki smiled, an apron around her waist and her hair piled on top of her head.

Cindy explained the plans for the day and pointed the soldiers toward the various activities. Families arrived, and soon the picnic area was bustling with smiling faces.

Later, the guys and gals had fun floating on the calm side of the lake, staying well away from the channel between Big Island and the smaller island to the south. Some of the more mobile soldiers climbed the tower and rode the zip line that hung between the two bodies of land. Beach volleyball games ran throughout the day and a fun run around the island was held with ambulatory soldiers helping those in wheelchairs.

Brody found himself partnered with Ted, and the two men began to have an understanding as they helped some of the handicapped guys with the various events.

Ted's laughter could be heard across the island, and a few times, Stephanie turned to watch her brother. A smile covered her face, something Brody had seen so rarely.

When she saw him staring at her, her smile wavered, and she turned back to whatever chore she was doing at the time.

As the afternoon waned, the men boated back to the marina to catch the bus that would take them to the barracks. Most of the families had returned earlier in the day.

Stephanie stood near a picnic bench, checking off the last of the supplies that were being loaded onto the military crafts.

"Did you get a chance to eat?" Brody asked.

"Nikki fixed something for me." Stephanie pointed to the untouched plate of food on the table.

Seeing an empty peanut oil container in the trash, Brody became concerned. "You can't eat the chicken if it was deep-fried in peanut oil, Stephanie. You need to be careful."

"Nikki grilled my chicken and didn't use oil."

"But you're still not eating it."

Turning away, she avoided his gaze. "I'll eat once I get home."

Although Stephanie sounded confident, she was probably fearful of having another allergic reaction. He stared at Nikki, who appeared in the door to the kitchen, wondering if she could have had something to do with the recent attacks.

Ted helped Cindy load the overflow items onto her boat. They were laughing and seemed to enjoy working together. Nikki walked toward them. The look she flashed Cindy was anything but friendly.

"The kitchen's clean and everything's packed away." She checked her watch. "I need to get back to the mainland. The Post Exchange gave me the afternoon off, but I have to work the evening shift."

Cindy jabbed a playful finger at Ted. "I'm trying to convince this guy to ride the zip line. What's with you, Ted? You've been working all day, and the picnic was for you."

His cheeks flushed. "I wanted to give Stephanie a hand."

"Everyone's left the island." Cindy pointed to the last military craft, heading back to the marina.

"Maybe Ted doesn't want to change into his swimsuit," Nikki said, an angry edge to her voice.

"Oh, come on, Nikki," Cindy mocked. "You never were the adventurous type."

Stephanie glanced at the tall tower and the rather bulky harness that had carried the soldiers along the thin cable. "You don't have to do anything you don't want to do, Ted."

"It's not a problem," he said, smiling back at Cindy. "Give me a minute to change."

By the time the supplies were loaded in Stephanie's boat, Ted had returned, wearing swim trucks and an army T-shirt. The scars on his legs showed the extent of his combat injuries.

Brody could only imagine the pain he had endured and the long months of healing that had bought Ted to this point.

"I'm not sure you should do the zip line, Ted," Stephanie cautioned. "Nikki needs to get back to the marina so she won't be late for work. Why don't you boat back with us?"

"Come on, Stephanie. Don't pull that mother routine on me."

She bristled. Brody hadn't expected the comment

and knew she hadn't, either. The look on her face revealed the pain her brother's words had caused.

"I'll stay with Ted if you want to take Nikki back," Brody volunteered. "Cindy can give us a ride to the mainland when he finishes riding the zip line."

Stephanie scanned the sky.

"Don't worry about the weather," Brody said.

"Storms come up quickly out here."

"Now look who's imagining the worst-case scenario."

She smiled, which was a good sign. "Okay, you're in charge. I'll take Nikki back with me."

"We'll be right behind you."

"Goodbye, Brody."

Stephanie's words hung in the air and made his heart heavy, as if she were bidding him a final farewell. The case was resolved. At least that's what everyone thought, so why would Brody continue to feel that the perpetrator was still on the loose?

After untying the moorings, Stephanie steered *The Princess* away from the dock. He watched her craft until it was a small spot on the horizon, then she turned a bend and disappeared from sight.

Brody glanced up at the zip line tower. Cindy had connected Ted into the harness. He glanced down to where Brody stood on the sandy shore. From the look on his face, Ted was having second thoughts about being up so high.

Raising his hands to his mouth, Brody shouted, "You can change your mind, Ted. You don't have to ride—"

Before he could complete his sentence, Cindy shoved Ted forward and activated the slide.

He screamed, which sent a chill down Brody's spine. The kid had been doing so well today. Hopefully, the rapid descent wouldn't set him back. Brody had assured Stephanie her brother would be all right.

With lightning speed, Ted sailed along the line and over the rough water with the strong currents that formed between the two islands. A dark cloud rolled in and hid the sun. For an instant, Brody's attention turned skyward.

He heard the second scream before he realized Ted had fallen into the whirling water below.

Cindy was racing down the hill to where Brody stood. "The harness must have snapped."

"Did you fasten it securely?"

"Of course."

"Let's take your boat." Brody raced toward Cindy's craft. "The current is forcing him out into the deep water."

To her credit, Cindy reacted quickly. Once away from shore, she gunned the engine and made straight for where Ted floundered in the water, still partially attached to the heavy harness.

"He's not the best of swimmers," she called to Brody. "You better go in and help him. I'll pull around and pick you both up."

A life preserver was in the back of the boat. Brody threw it into the water. "Grab hold, Ted. It'll keep you afloat until I get to you."

Ted clutched the white ring, but the look on his face told Brody he needed to get to him fast.

After emptying his pockets, Brody toed off his shoes. He threw his cell phone to Cindy. "Call nine-one-one. Tell them to send an ambulance and rescue personnel."

He dove into the water. Surfacing some feet away from the boat, he kept his eyes on Ted as he used a modified Australian crawl to cover the distance from the boat to Ted.

The sound of the throttle made him glance back. Cindy had turned the craft and was barreling straight toward him.

"Stop," he shouted, raising his arm. Surely she could see him in the water.

The look on her face chilled him.

"I'm going to kill both of you," she shouted over the roar of the engine.

An icy thread of fear wove its way along Brody's spine. The police had arrested the wrong person. Keith Allen wasn't the killer. Cindy was.

Diving deep, Brody saved himself from being run down. Once he surfaced again, he watched her turn the craft around. At least, she wasn't aiming for Ted, who floated on the life preserver about fifty feet away.

"You killed Paul." Brody needed information.

"And I would have killed Joshua, except Stephanie called his house and said she was on the way. I wanted him to drown like Hayden had."

"You drugged Stephanie and tried to drown her."

"She would have died except for you. You won't be

able to save her this time because I'll make sure you're dead. Ted won't survive long in the water."

"Why, Cindy?"

"Because Hayden loved me. He told me that day on the lake, just before he jumped into the water after me. Stephanie saved everyone except him. She never liked Hayden because of what his mother had done. He was everything Ted should have been and wasn't. Stephanie was always so protective of her brother. She tried to be his mother and that upset him even more. He didn't want a second mother, he wanted his dad. But his father never had time for him." Brody tried to follow her ramblings.

Before he could ask about Hazel and what she had done, Cindy pushed on the throttle.

"The storm clouds are moving in," she screamed. "I'll make sure you won't survive." Her face twisted with rage, her teeth clenched together, her eyes wide.

Brody glanced at Ted, floating away from the path of the craft. Hopefully, Cindy would keep going to the marina, thinking Ted would perish in the rapidly churning water.

The boat approached. Sucking in a lungful of air, Brody dove deep but not deep enough. The rotor caught his leg, cutting a deep gash into his flesh. Blood swirled from the wound and floated to the surface.

The engine wound down. Hopefully, Cindy saw the blood. His chest burned, but he remained submerged. The longer he stayed below water, the more likely she would think he had perished.

His lungs screamed for air.

Another second and they would surely explode.

The sound of the engine came at the moment he surfaced.

He gulped air.

A crash of thunder sounded overhead.

Cindy glanced back. Once again, Brody dove underwater and surfaced as the craft headed for the mainland. He turned to search for Ted, but in the growing darkness and the rising crest of the waves, he could see only the water and the lightning that zigzagged across the sky.

TWENTY-TWO

Noticing the darkening sky, Stephanie hurried to unload the rest of the supplies. She had sent Nikki back to post so she wouldn't be late for work.

Glancing first at her watch and then at the water, she expected to see Cindy's boat bringing Ted and Brody back to the marina. Ready to set out to find them, she let out a pent-up breath when the boat rounded the bend.

Stephanie knew the relief she was feeling was not just for Ted but also for Brody. He'd helped in so many ways today, and she'd taken comfort seeing how he and Ted had worked together, whether hauling supplies or aiding some of the other, more seriously wounded soldiers. They'd even formed a team for the fun run and had pushed two other men in wheelchairs.

Although the foursome hadn't won the timed awards, they'd come first in the wheelchair competition with a bevy of high fives around. Seeing the sense of accomplishment on Ted's face when he and Brody stood together with their handicapped teammates had made her reconsider what she had thought about Brody. Perhaps there was hope for them after all.

Knowing she was getting ahead of herself, Stephanie carried the last box of supplies to her car. When she returned to the dock, she saw Cindy tying up her boat.

A tingle of concern gave her pause as she looked around the empty marina. "Where are Ted and Brody?"

"They stayed behind. One of the other soldiers came by with his boat. Ted wanted another turn on the zip line."

Stephanie glanced at the lightning in the distance. The strikes had to be hitting close to Big Island. "The zip line is the last place he should be in this storm."

Cindy's smile was reassuring. "I'm sure they're headed back by now." She pointed to the water. "They're probably right around the bend. I wouldn't worry, Stephanie."

But she *was* worried and also angry that Cindy had returned to the marina without them.

"Who's the soldier?"

"I can't remember his name. He was there today. I saw you talking to him. Big guy. Brown hair, cut in a military buzz."

Which would fit most of the guys at the picnic. "Sam Taylor?"

"That's him. He should be here in a minute or two."

Cindy stepped closer and stared at Stephanie's face. "You forgot to use sunscreen."

Stephanie touched her cheeks, knowing they were probably pink. "I was too busy."

"I've got some great aloe that takes the sting out of

any sunburn and also helps so you won't peel." She dug in her purse and pulled out an unmarked plastic spray bottle. "I buy it in a large size and then keep the smaller atomizer in my purse." She sprayed a hefty dose over Stephanie's face.

Stepping back, she groaned and wiped her hand over her lips. "It got in my mouth, and it tastes terrible, Cindy, and smells even worse. I think I inhaled half the bottle."

"You've got some on your cheeks that needs to be rubbed in. It's grainy but effective."

The spray wasn't cooling or pleasant. Stephanie shook her head. "That's enough. Thanks."

"Here's a tote one of the ladies left on the island." Cindy handed the bag to Stephanie. "The name tag on the outside says it belongs to Maureen Meyers. Could you see she gets it?"

"Maureen's the wife of one of the soldiers. Sure, I'll drop it off at her quarters when I'm back on post."

Cindy glanced at her watch. "I've got to hurry. Walt wanted me to join him for dinner, and I don't want to keep him waiting."

Once again, Stephanie turned her gaze to the choppy water. "Cindy, are you sure Sam was heading back to the marina?"

"Of course. He'll be here in a minute or two."

With a wave of her hand, Cindy raced to her car and soon left the marina.

With a frustrated sigh, Stephanie grabbed her purse and hurried to the end of the walkway where she scanned the lot, hoping to see Sam Taylor's Hummer.

Even used, the vehicle was much too expensive and had probably soaked up all Sam's reenlistment bonuses and monthly paychecks, as well as his hazardous duty pay while he was deployed.

The Hummer wasn't in the marina lot.

From the top of the walkway, she could see Big Island in the distance with no boats in sight. What she did see was the descending darkness, and a sheet of rain heading across the lake toward the marina.

Whatever had happened wasn't good.

She raced toward *The Princess,* but it was too slow and too small to navigate the choppy waters. She had to take *The Upton Queen.*

The boat she hadn't been in since the night Hayden died.

Tonight Ted was in danger as well as Brody. She needed to get to Big Island as quickly as possible.

"Oh, please, God. Help me save both of them, so no one else has to die."

TWENTY-THREE

"Mayday, Mayday." Stephanie repeated the distress alert over the cabin cruiser's radio. Once she received a response, she relayed her location and that she needed help on Big Island Lake.

Glancing at the gas gauge, she realized too late the tank was riding on empty. She had to make it to the island. From there, she could wait out the storm as long as she knew Ted and Brody were safe.

The wind howled and rain pummeled the craft. Giant waves splashed against the bow, rocking the vessel and causing her to worry whether the boat would survive the forceful winds and vicious surf.

Once again, she was back three years ago. She'd forbidden Ted to go to the Big Island with the rest of the kids. He'd promised her he would spend the day with Paul at his house.

Stephanie had taken his compliance as a good sign and was relieved that her work with Ted was starting to pay off. She decided to show him how happy she was about his change of heart and had prepared a carrot cake, which was his favorite. He'd called while she was making the cream cheese icing. First he'd told her where he was and then that he and the others needed a ride back to the marina.

Keith had said he would pick them up, but he had gone to Atlanta and was tied up getting out of the city. Stephanie had done so much and was so tired of failing with her brother, she refused to ruin the cake, plus she wanted him to realize how disappointed she was with his decision to go with the kids instead of obeying her.

So she had waited thirty minutes until the cake was done and sitting on the counter before she left the house, angry and ready to give her brother a piece of her mind.

Her delay that day had caused Hayden's death. She could never forgive herself. Now this evening, she couldn't let another mistake cost someone else's life.

Not her brother's. Not Brody's.

God had failed to respond to her pleas for help three years ago. If only He would listen to her now.

"Ted! Brody!" she screamed as she approached the island. She turned on the spotlight and rotated it back and forth, searching for some sign of them. Raising her hands to her lips, she called their names repeatedly as she played the spotlight over the shore, seeing nothing.

Needing something with more volume, she rang the bell, hoping its deep knell would be heard over the thunder and roar of the wind.

Adjusting the angle of the light, she saw something on the swell in the distance and steered forward. There in the light was Ted, desperately hanging on to the life preserver. He raised his hand and shouted back to her.

Tears of relief burned her eyes. She edged near him and stretched out her hand.

Once on board, he pointed to the water. "Brody and I got separated. I thought I heard him call my name."

The wind whipped at her hair. She pushed it back and squinted into the murky water, looking for any sign of Brody as she turned the spotlight into the deep, dark abyss.

"Where is he?" she screamed above the storm.

"There." Ted pointed to where the light cut through the night.

Was that a hand? Without thought, she dove into the water, following the light.

But she couldn't find Brody.

She swam deeper, reaching for anything she saw that could be him, his hand, his arm.

Her lungs burned.

She surfaced, grabbed another breath and dove again, just as she had done so many times in her dreams.

Please, God. Let me find him.

Ted adjusted the light, and she dove again, only this time, as her lungs burned for oxygen, a vision from her past appeared. Something she had seen that night as she labored to save Hayden. Something she had glimpsed too briefly to recognize in her dreams. A memory from her past she had buried as a child when she had walked in on Aunt Hazel in her parents' bedroom. With her youthful innocence, she hadn't realized the significance of finding her father in bed with her mother's sister.

Gasping for air, Stephanie surfaced, upset by the vision as well as her inability to find Brody.

"There he is," Ted screamed.

She saw Brody's shirt. Grabbing him, she pulled him close. Ted threw the life preserver that was attached to the craft by a rope and pulled them toward the boat. Between them pushing and lifting, they hoisted Brody on deck.

Stephanie placed her hands under his sternum and pressed down, as he had done to her just a few days earlier. One, two, three, the pace was fast, and she used her full weight to keep his blood circulating.

"Radio for help," she called to Ted, "and head for the marina."

The engine throttled forward and the craft moved through the water. Then, like a dying creature, it sputtered and stopped. The rain eased ever so slightly, but fog floated in around them.

"We ran out of gas," Ted called to her through the haze.

"What about the radio?"

"It's not working."

"Ring the bell, Ted. Someone might hear us."

Her brother scrambled to the stern and began to ring the death dirge.

Stephanie had found Brody, but that didn't mean she'd be able to save him.

Brody's chest burned like fire. A weight crashed into his ribs, and he gasped for air.

Turning his head to the side, he gagged. Water spewed from his mouth.

"Oh, Brody, you're alive."

He didn't feel alive—he felt battered and broken, until he blinked his eyes open and saw Stephanie's face just inches from his own.

"Talk to me," she begged. "Tell me you're okay."

"I—I'm o-okay."

A smile covered her mouth, a mouth he wanted to kiss, but he'd have to wait until he could catch his breath and sit up without feeling dizzy and sick.

"Head for the marina," he said.

She shook her head. "We've run out of gas."

"Call for help."

"We have." Yet the call had gone unanswered.

At least the rain had stopped, and although the waves were high, the craft could handle the rough surf. If only her stomach could. She'd never gotten seasick before. She hung her head. The world swirled around her.

Her cheeks were on fire. Not sunburn; something worse. What had been in the aloe spray?

"Are you all right?" Brody sat up and reached for her.

As much as Stephanie wanted to reassure him, all she could do was gasp for air.

"Stephanie!" Brody screamed. Her cheeks were beet red and burning hot.

"She's having a reaction," he called to Ted. "Get the EpiPen out of her purse."

Grabbing the shoulder bag, Ted dumped the contents on the deck. Her wallet and lipstick. A package of tissues and a comb. He shook the purse again. Two plastic EpiPen cases fell onto the deck. "Stay calm, honey. The epinephrine will work in a minute or two."

Her raspy pull for air sent a rush of terror that knotted his stomach. His hands couldn't undo the packaging fast enough.

When he held up the first Auto-Injector, he saw something that made his heart sink. The vial was spent. He opened the second EpiPen and found it empty, too.

"Radio for help again," he told Ted. "This time you've got to get through."

Stephanie's whole body convulsed. She needed more air than her constricted bronchioles would allow.

"Did your mother keep any medication onboard?" Brody asked Ted.

"In the first-aid kit." He raced below deck and returned with the box that he opened and then held out for Brody, who rummaged through the gauze and tape. His fingers dug to the bottom and found nothing.

"Mom kept a small pouch in a cubbyhole under one of the seats. It may still be there."

Brody took Stephanie's hand. Her chest heaved as she tried to draw in the oxygen she so desperately needed.

Ted raced to the stern and returned carrying two plastic containers. "They're out-of-date."

"Then say a prayer that they'll still work."

Uncapping the first applicator, Brody sighed with relief when he saw the medication had not been depleted. In one swift motion, he jabbed the spring-loaded syringe into her thigh.

"Get the next one ready, Ted."

Brody bent over Stephanie, searching for any change in her condition. The wild look in her eyes told him the terrible truth. She still struggled to breathe. The epinephrine must be too old to counter the reaction.

"Please, God." He reached for the second EpiPen.

Once again, he pushed the injector firmly against her thigh. The medication automatically released. If only it would work.

Stephanie continued to gasp for air.

Seeing her distress, Brody feared that he was going to lose her, and without Stephanie, he couldn't go on.

The sound of the ship's bell rang in the fog of her mind. Stephanie couldn't focus or pull herself out of the haze.

Voices sounded around her.

"Can you hear me? Open your eyes, hon."

She inhaled deeply, enjoying the clean air that filled her lungs. The burning had ended, along with the fear of not being able to breathe.

She lifted her hand toward her face.

"Watch, honey. You're getting oxygen. You're probably feeling the nasal cannula."

Could she be dreaming? Her struggle for air had been so severe.

Someone touched her arm. "Stephanie, open your eyes."

Brody's voice. She wasn't dreaming. Thank God, she was alive.

With another deep inhale, she forced her eyes to blink open. A spotlight caused her to turn her head in order to shield her eyes.

"Move the light," Brody warned. "The glare's too much for her."

She sensed him leaning in closer and felt his warm breath on her cheek. "Now, hon. You can open your eyes."

Once again, she blinked her eyes open and was rewarded with seeing his face close to hers.

"Oh, Stephanie." His voice was husky with emotion. "I thought I'd lost you."

"Br…Brody." She sighed, then inhaled again, comforted by the restorative power of the oxygen-rich air. She didn't need to look at Brody's drawn face to know how close she'd come to not surviving.

"Ted?" She turned her head, searching for him. A number of boatmen and a few medical personnel huddled close by. A stab of fear made her try to sit up.

"I'm right here, sis." He stuck his head over Brody's shoulder.

Her brother smiled, a wide and heartfelt grin she hadn't seen in so long. He rested his hand on Brody's shoulder, and the two guys exchanged looks that told her a bond had formed between them.

"How…how are you, Ted?"

"Fine, Steph, now that you came back to join us."

"But—" She didn't understand his comment.

"You went to another place. We didn't think you'd come back to life. Mom's old EpiPens kicked in and gave you enough medication to open your airway ever so slightly."

He glanced at the men joining them on the deck. "These guys arrived in time to do the rest of the treatment. They've assured us you're going to be okay."

"Cindy…sprayed my face. I breathed it in. It must have contained…" She couldn't go on. The thought of what Cindy had done brought back memories of that day on the water three years ago.

Brody quickly recounted what Cindy had told him about loving Hayden and wanting to avenge his death.

"She was angry that all of us lived when he didn't," Ted added. "Hayden liked to flirt. He had given her the wrong impression, which cost Paul his life."

"What about Joshua?"

"We'll find out how he's doing as soon as we get back to the mainland. The chief of police is searching for Cindy."

The fog had lifted somewhat by the time they neared the marina. Two of the men stepped to the front of the boat to talk to Ted. Stephanie sat next to Brody. He wrapped his arm around her shoulder and pulled her close. She continued to think about Cindy's vindictive actions. The aloe spray must have contained ground nuts, just as they'd found in the raisins.

In a flash of clarity, Stephanie remembered the tote.

Her heart pounded a warning when she realized they were still in danger.

She grabbed Brody's hand. "Stop the boat. We can't dock."

"An ambulance is ready to transport you to the hospital. You're going to be okay, honey."

"No." She shook her head. "You don't understand. Cindy said one of the wives had left a tote at the picnic. She insisted I take it back to post, but it's still on my boat."

Brody's eyes locked on hers. His smile disappeared and was replaced with the keen gaze of a law-enforcement officer.

"Don't enter the marina, Ted. There could be a bomb on that small craft." Brody pointed to *The Princess,* then looked down at Stephanie. "Where's the tote?"

"In the front. It's a yellow cloth bag decorated with fabric flowers."

The lead cop called headquarters. "Send the bomb crew and make sure the marina is sealed off. If this baby blows, I don't want anyone else injured." He nodded, the phone still at his ear. "We'll head for the small dock south of here. I'll have the ambulance meet us there."

Two patrol cars quickly arrived and secured the marina. The police boat that had come to their rescue remained a distance out from shore. Once the bomb crew was in place, the boat followed *The Upton Queen* to the smaller dock and met up with Brody there.

"Chief Palmer said he wants to talk to you, sir." One of the officers held out his phone to Brody.

The police chief came over the line. "We've got her. Cindy was holed up in the large prefab warehouse she erected on her property. She's got her own makeshift garage out there. Evidently, she learned mechanics from her brother. Plus, you'll never guess what was parked inside."

"A souped-up truck with mud tires, red in color."

"You've got that right. She took an old, used pickup and repainted it, added mud tires and rebuilt the engine. She wanted it to look just like Hayden's Ford. Here's the strange part. She claimed to be able to feel his presence when she drove the truck around her property. The woman's deranged, in my opinion, but we'll let a court of law determine what they want to do with her. She had one area of her warehouse turned into a shrine of sorts to Hayden's memory. High school photos, memorabilia. It gave me the creeps."

"Did she admit to nearly sideswiping Stephanie outside Joshua's subdivision?"

"When she accessed Josh's voice mail and heard that Stephanie was en route to his house, she had to change her plans and nearly ran Ms. Upton off the road while trying to get away."

"It appeared to me that she hit Joshua from behind and planned to drown him in the tub."

"That's what she admitted doing, although not in nice terms. She kept railing that Ms. Upton shouldn't have come back. Cindy had wanted to take her time with her revenge, but when she saw Ted's sister, she knew she had to act fast."

"She was in love with Hayden Allen and felt Stephanie had left him to perish intentionally."

The chief whistled over the phone. "That explains the additional photos we found. Some shots she probably took when Hayden wasn't looking. If you ask my opinion, Cindy made up a fictional world where the boyfriend still existed and still loved her."

"I'm not sure how he felt about her, Chief. That could have made the problem even worse." Brody shook his head, thinking of all the pain Cindy had caused. If only she had gotten help. Counseling, psychiatric care, medication to aid her in overcoming the trauma of losing the boy she supposedly loved. Unfortunately, she'd kept everything inside.

"Have you talked to Walt Ferrol?" Brody asked.

"He's hiring a lawyer and plans to fight the charges against his sister. From the looks of things, the case is airtight. Plus, she said she wants to write down what happened so folks will realize why she had to hurt Joshua and kill Paul."

"She almost killed Ted and Stephanie, too."

"I heard she ran you down in the water. She thought you and Ted had both perished. When I told her you survived, she broke down and cried. And not for joy."

"The EMTs are ready to transport Stephanie to the hospital. I'm going with her."

"Thank her for what she did. Once again, we owe her a debt of gratitude."

"I don't think she wants a fuss made, Chief."

"Maybe not, but her heroism needs to be recognized. You need recognition, as well."

"Negative. Just call my boss and tell him you appreciate the way the CID helped on this investigation."

"You've got it. Anytime you want to leave the military and settle down, say with a pretty local gal, come see me about a job in law enforcement."

Brody appreciated the offer.

"I mean it. I could use a good man like you."

He smiled as he disconnected and then limped to the ambulance. The EMT raised an eyebrow when he climbed in the rear.

Brody held up his hand. "CID from Fort Rickman. It's incumbent on me to remain with the patient."

The guy smiled and nodded. "Yes, sir. I never mess with the cops. Plus—" He glanced down at Brody's leg. "Looks like that cut should be treated at the E.R. I'll leave you two back here. My partner and I will ride up front. Just call out if you need anything."

The door shut, and Brody took Stephanie's hand. He would explain what the chief of police had said later. Right now, he wanted to reassure her everything was going to be all right.

"Ted's driving my car to the hospital."

Her eyes widened. "You trust him?"

"After what we've been through, I trust him with my life."

"And my life, Brody? Do you trust him with that, as well?"

He nodded. "Maybe I was too hard on Ted at first, but he was in a bad place and had a lot to deal with.

Hopefully, what we all faced today made him realize life goes on and the past is behind him."

"Is that something you've learned?"

He nodded, leaning closer to her. "I'm only thinking of the present moment and having the doctor check you out and give you a clean bill of health."

"So…" She rolled her eyes and stuck out her lower lip in a pretend pout. "You're not thinking about the future at all?"

"Okay, you're right." He laughed. "I am thinking about asking you out for dinner and taking you to a nice restaurant, and then maybe we can stroll along the river's edge, especially if it's a moonlit night with the stars twinkling overhead."

She sighed. "That sounds delightful."

"We could stop in a secluded spot, and then I could take you in my arms and pull you close so that all I could see would be your beautiful face bathed in moonlight."

"What would happen then?" she teased.

"Then I'd kiss you. Just like this."

He lowered his lips to hers and felt a rush of emotion fill him as the two of them were joined. He wove his hand through her hair and held her close, never wanting anything to separate them again.

They had been through so much, and he had almost lost her too many times, but all that was behind them. Lisa had died by the hand of a man who was confused and suffering, just as Cindy was suffering in her own way.

Being with Stephanie healed the pain of Brody's

past. Hopefully, she realized Hayden's death was in no way her fault. She had her brother back, and Brody, at long last, was able to see the good in him and had hope for his future as well as their own.

As he drew away, he heard her sigh, and his heart skittered in his chest. "I don't want to leave you, ever, Stephanie."

"Oh, Brody."

Once again, he lowered his lips to hers and continued to kiss her as the ambulance raced toward the hospital and the siren screeched in the night.

TWENTY-FOUR

Stephanie and Brody attended church on post the next morning. Ted and Nikki joined them there. After the service, they visited Joshua in the hospital. His condition had improved, and he'd been moved from the ICU into a private room.

Ted and Nikki stayed with their friend while Brody drove Stephanie to Magnolia Manor. Earlier, she had arranged to meet Keith at the nursing home.

"Are you sure you feel up to this?" Keith asked her as they approached.

She nodded. "Have you said anything to Aunt Hazel?"

"Only that you've come back to town."

"Does she know you were taken into custody?"

He shook his head. "Luckily, no. The nursing-home staff didn't want to upset her, which I appreciated."

She touched his arm. "I'm sorry about what happened, Keith."

He glanced from Stephanie to Brody. "Everything worked out in the end. No one realized Cindy had access to so many places in town through her mother's cleaning business. The real-estate office, the bakery—"

"And my parent's house," Stephanie added. "My mother started using the cleaning service when she was pregnant with Ted. Her morning sickness for the first three months was severe. She needed help around the house and even went into the hospital for dehydration during that time. I was at home with my father."

Keith nodded. "That's when you walked in on your dad and my mother."

"Only I blanked out the memory. I was six years old and didn't understand what I was seeing. When I was searching for Hayden, the memory returned ever so briefly. Yesterday, as I was looking for Brody, I saw everything in a flash of awareness."

Stephanie hesitated for a moment and then added, "Their affair occurred around the time your mother became pregnant, Keith. Do you know who Hayden's father was?"

He shook his head. "I've never asked and never needed to know. Either way, Hayden was still my brother."

"And a very special guy." Stephanie turned to Brody. "You said Cindy's mom was aware of what was going on?"

"Evidently, at some point, she shared what she knew with her daughter."

"My dad continued using the cleaning service after my mother died," Stephanie said. "Cindy made a duplicate house key. Dad had provided the security code so the cleaning team could get into the house even when he had set the alarm."

"Unfortunately, no one realized the bitterness Cindy harbored." Keith glanced at the nursing home. "Are you ready?"

Stephanie hesitated. "There's one thing I never understood, Keith. Did you go to Atlanta that day?"

He nodded. "I wanted to leave Freemont. A job opened up in the city. I went for the interview and would have had plenty of time to get back, but they asked me to talk to some more people in the company that afternoon. I called Mother and asked her to pick up the kids."

"But…but she didn't?"

"I'm not sure what happened. She may have been having ministrokes at that time and forgot I had even called. Not long after Hayden's death, she had her first major attack. I was offered the job but turned it down so I could take care of her."

Stephanie hadn't realized the depth of compassion in Keith's heart. "You never told anyone about calling her."

He shook his head. "My mother had enough guilt to carry. She didn't need me pointing a finger at her."

"You're a good man," she said with sincerity.

"Thanks, Stephanie. That means a lot to me."

She turned to Brody and squeezed his hand. "We won't be long."

"I'll be waiting."

Together, she and Keith entered the nursing home

and headed for Aunt Hazel's room. She was propped up in bed, staring at the door through which they entered.

She tried to smile. Her lips sagged with the effort, but her eyes were bright and full of welcome.

"Mama, look who's come to visit you." Keith motioned Stephanie forward.

She neared the bed and took Aunt Hazel's hand. "I've missed you."

Which was true. After her own mother's death, she and Aunt Hazel had drawn closer. But ever since Hayden had died, Stephanie hadn't been able to face the grieving mother. She'd gone to his funeral but left without talking to her aunt.

Hazel gripped Stephanie's hand and struggled to form her words. "You…you're…home."

"I'm working at Fort Rickman, Aunt Hazel, so I'll be able to visit you often."

The woman smiled.

"Keith is a wonderful son," Stephanie continued. "You have so much to be proud of."

Again Hazel nodded, but her face clouded as if she was remembering her own loss.

"Hayden was a wonderful son, too." Stephanie hesitated before adding, "I always thought of him as a brother."

The woman's eyes widened ever so slightly.

Stephanie nodded with understanding. "For a long time, I shut God out of my life, but I've realized the Lord was waiting with open arms for me to return to Him. We've all made mistakes. If we're truly sorry, we need to ask His forgiveness."

She glanced up at Keith before she continued. "Don't dwell on the past, but be grateful for what you have today."

Hazel's eyes watered and a tear ran down her cheek. She released Stephanie's hand and reached for Keith's. Stepping back, Stephanie watched as he sat on the side of his mother's bed. Hazel's mouth moved as she struggled to talk.

"I know, Mama," Keith soothed. "I love you, too."

Dear God, bless this mother and son with the fullness of Your love and mercy.

Knowing they had much to reconcile, Stephanie left the nursing home. Outside, the sun was shining, and the sky was bright.

Brody was standing by his car, waiting for her, just as he had promised.

She walked into his arms, feeling that special connection, a sense of coming home that wiped away the burdens she had carried for too long and filled her with an anticipation and expectation of what the future could hold. A future with Brody.

"Are you okay?" he asked.

She nodded. "Now I need to call my father."

"What are you going to say?"

"That Ted and I are waiting for him to come home."

Brody hugged her even more tightly. "I'm proud of you."

She shook her head. "It's not me. It's what the Lord revealed to me during all this. I was thinking only of myself by carrying the guilt for Hayden's death. Looking inward, I didn't realize so many other folks were struggling, as well."

She pulled back ever so slightly. "At the hospital, Ted told me he had talked Hayden into bringing the alcohol that day. All this time, Ted felt he was responsible for what happened. He closed me out of his life, knowing if he had done what I had asked, Hayden might still be alive. Ted asked my forgiveness, and for the first time in three years, we hugged and cried and…and healed."

"I'm so glad."

"He's determined to follow through with counseling. Nikki's been encouraging him. I think she's a good influence on him."

"And you're a good influence on me. There's something in the car I want to show you."

Brody reached into the backseat and pulled out a sketch pad. "I've started drawing again." He flipped the pages and stopped at a charcoal sketch of the lake with a boat—*The Upton Queen*—sailing toward the rising sun.

"You've faced your fears, Stephanie, just as I faced mine. If it wasn't for the past, I never would have gone into the CID, and you never would have taken the job at Fort Rickman. But because of what happened to both of us, we found each other."

She smiled. "The sketch is beautiful, Brody." She pointed to the boat. "You even included the maritime bell."

"I titled it 'New Day Dawning.'"

She nodded, appreciating the significance for both

of them. A new day, a fresh start, a lifetime waiting for them to share together.

"Let's take a drive," she suggested.

"Where?"

"Someplace special."

It didn't take Brody long to realize where they were headed. Stephanie directed him through town, where they picked up a picnic lunch, and then to the open road that led to the place she had most dreaded at one time. A place that had been tragic as well as redemptive, providing the healing that she and Ted had needed.

Brody pulled into the marina and held the car door for her. She grabbed her purse and the bag containing their lunch.

"You've got your new EpiPens, don't you?"

She smiled. "Two of them, as well as the keys to *The Upton Queen*."

They untied the moorings and headed out of the marina, where Stephanie turned the controls over to him. Brody steered the craft away from Big Island and then eased back on the throttle. Letting the boat rock gently on the waves, he turned to face Stephanie.

"I know your mother must have been a beautiful woman."

Stephanie tilted her head.

"Because she had such a beautiful daughter."

Smiling, she took his hand. "She must have known about Dad's affair with Hazel, but she stayed with him.

She was always so forgiving. I wanted to be more like her, but I seemed to have my father's practicality."

"A mix that's perfect in my eyes."

"You know so little about me," she said.

"I know you're strong and determined, and when you care for someone, you'll do anything to help them. I know you've made me think about the future instead of the past, and that when I'm with you the day seems brighter."

He wrapped his arms around her and drew her closer. "I know we haven't known each other long in terms of time, but—"

She stared at him, her eyes wide.

"But I love you more than anything, and—"

"Oh, Brody."

"I know, I know," he said. "We need to take it one day at a time."

She smiled. "I'd like that."

"Really?"

"Cross my heart."

She laughed and playfully kissed his lips. Pulling back, the laughter in her eyes changed, and he saw the love he had been hoping she would feel for him. He drew her closer and lowered his lips to hers, feeling at home with her in his arms.

At some point, they ate. Brody never wanted to stop being with Stephanie, so the boat lolled on the lake until the sun was starting to set.

Pulling back into the marina, they laughed at the gulls overhead. The breeze caught Stephanie's hair, brushing it across Brody's face. He turned again to capture her lips, never wanting the day to end.

But as they walked together back to his car, he knew they'd have more days, so many more. With the setting sun would come the promise of tomorrow and a new day dawning. A new day filled with love and hope, filled with Stephanie.

EPILOGUE

"I don't remember November ever being this warm," Stephanie said as she placed a basket of potato chips on the glass-topped patio table.

Nikki opened the ice bucket and dropped three cubes into her insulated plastic glass. "I'm glad you had this get-together." She glanced at Ted, sitting next to Brody in the wrought-iron chairs near the pool. "The two guys have become such good friends. Ted told me Brody's like an older brother."

"He's a good role model, which is what Ted needed. The counselor keeps praising his progress."

"I'm glad you came back to Freemont, Stephanie." The younger woman paused, her expression suddenly serious. "Ted needed you, even if he didn't realize it."

"That goes both ways. I needed him, as well."

"And your dad?"

"He's working on being a father, which is a huge change."

"Ted said he's in Europe again."

"But it's just a short trip this time. He insisted we use his house for the gathering today." Stephanie laughed. "He knew my apartment was too small for a Veterans Day party."

Nikki poured iced tea into the glass she held. "Anything I can do to help?"

"Everything's done. Enjoy the afternoon."

Nikki walked to where Ted sat by the pool. Brody offered her his chair and then joined Stephanie at the table.

"You're working too hard," he said, reaching for her hand.

She wrapped her fingers through his, appreciating his concern for her well-being. "Thanks for arriving early and getting the patio ready." Glancing at the sunny sky, she added, "Even Mother Nature cooperated so we could be outdoors. The weather is perfect."

"When do you want me to start the grill?"

"After a few more of the guests arrive. I invited Ted's care team and Major Jenkins. They should be here shortly, along with some of the other folks from work."

"What about Josh?"

"He asked if he could bring a friend."

Brody raised his brow. "A girl?"

Stephanie nodded. "She works with Nikki at the Post Exchange. They seem to be hitting it off."

"I'm glad. Josh is a good guy."

"Keith offered him a job managing some of the rental properties in town as soon as his discharge from the army comes through. Josh is telling everyone he's only got a few weeks left on active duty."

Ted's smart phone rang. He pulled it to his ear and nodded. "You can do it, buddy."

Hanging up, he grabbed Nikki's hand. "That was Josh. He's out front and has a surprise for us." The young couple left the patio and rounded the house.

Stephanie started after them, but Brody pulled her back into his arms. "We're alone, at least for a few minutes. I wanted to tell you how beautiful you look today."

"We had to be alone for you to pay me a compliment?" she teased.

His upper lip twitched. "I also wanted a kiss."

She stepped closer and snuggled more deeply into his arms. Looking up, she raised her brow. "What are you waiting for?"

He smiled ever so slightly and then his expression changed. What she saw in his eyes made her breath hitch. She waited for what seemed like an eternity as he slowly—ever so slowly—dropped his lips to hers.

Fireworks.

She saw red, white and blue fireworks even though her eyes were closed. Her heart seemed to explode with joy at the same time her knees went weak.

Luckily, Brody was supporting her.

"You've been kissing me for three months, Special Agent Goodman," she said as their lips parted.

"Yes, ma'am."

"And I still get goose bumps even on a warm day."

"So you like my kisses?" His eyes twinkled.

"I like everything about you."

"Funny, but I feel the same about you." He hesitated, his gaze even more intense. "It's not the right time, is it?"

She tried to calm the excitement bubbling within her. "Sometimes you just have to seize the moment."

"You know what I'm thinking?"

She shrugged innocently. "Are you thinking about kissing me again?"

"I'm thinking about spending the rest of my life with you."

She blinked. "Really?"

"Really? But only if that sounds good to you."

She nodded, unable to put words to the emotion welling up inside her.

"I don't want to rush you. We'll do it the right way, with dinner and candlelight."

"A day on the lake would also work."

He nodded. "We could do both."

"I got Dad's permission to change the name of *The Princess.*"

"New Day Dawning?"

"It's a perfect fit."

"Just like us."

He kissed her again and time stood still. When she eventually pulled back, she glanced over her shoulder to see Ted and Nikki, standing with Josh, who was wearing his new prosthetic legs. Next to him stood a petite blonde who gripped his hand.

Keith came up behind them. "Did I miss something?"

Ted laughed. "Only if Brody and Stephanie have some good news to share."

"You'll be the first to know," Stephanie said with a wink.

Brody shook Joshua's hand after he had walked across the patio, his gait slow but steady. "Way to go, Josh."

"Thank you, sir." He introduced his girlfriend, who smiled briefly at Brody and then turned her gaze back to Josh.

The military and civilians from the Warrior Transitional Battalion arrived and seemed to enjoy the afternoon. By nightfall, most of them had said their goodbyes.

Josh and his girlfriend had left earlier, along with Keith, who planned to visit his mom at the nursing home. Ted and Nikki helped with the cleanup and then returned to the patio to watch the sunset.

"We need a new way to celebrate the good times," he told Stephanie when she and Brody joined them there. "In the past, I rang the maritime bell when I was filled with pain, but today, I'm bursting with happiness." He smiled at Nikki and then back at Stephanie.

She understood the way her brother felt. "Like you, I'm ready for a fresh start, Ted."

He and Nikki walked to the bell. Ted grabbed the cord and pulled. The sound was sweet as it filled the night, like a church bell calling worshippers to prayer and a reminder of the healing power of love.

As the sun set on the horizon, the bell continued to ring. Brody wrapped Stephanie in his arms and pulled her close. She could feel the steady beat of his heart and the strength of his embrace.

She had come home to help her brother and had found Brody. She had also found her lost faith. Tomorrow a new day would dawn, filled with the promise of God's many blessings.

A man to love, a formal proposal and a wedding in the future. On post or in the little brick church on Third Street, she wasn't sure, just so she and Brody could be joined together in a covenant of love with the Lord, but she was getting ahead of herself. Right now she had something very important to do.

She rose on tiptoe, her lips so close to his. "I love you, Brody," she whispered.

"Oh, Stephanie, I love you more than my own life. You're my today, my tomorrow, my forever." He hesitated, staring into her eyes. "You're my everything."

Then he kissed her, and once again fireworks illuminated the sky, only this time over the golf course to celebrate Veterans Day. With Brody, every day would be special; every day would be a celebration.

As the bell pealed and the fireworks showered them in light, Stephanie stood wrapped in Brody's arms, breathing in the essence of the man she loved and would love until the end of time.

* * * * *

Dear Reader,

I hope you enjoyed THE SOLDIER'S SISTER, the fifth book in my Military Investigations Series, which features heroes and heroines in the army's Criminal Investigation Division. Each story stands alone so you can read them in any order, either in print or as an ebook: THE OFFICER'S SECRET, book 1; THE CAPTAIN'S MISSION, book 2; THE COLONEL'S DAUGHTER, book 3; and THE GENERAL'S SECRETARY, book 4.

I spent time with two AW2 advocates when I was researching this book: Nancy Carlisle and Ann Yingling. Both women care deeply about our wounded heroes and are working to improve their quality of life. I applaud all who reach out to our service members, and hope those of you reading this story will find ways to support returning military personnel in your local area.

I want to hear from you. Email me at *debby@debbygiusti.com* or write me c/o Love Inspired, 233 Broadway, Suite 1001, New York, NY, 10279.

Visit my website at *www.DebbyGiusti.com* and blog with me at *www.seekerville.blogspot.com*, *www.craftieladiesofromance.blogspot.com* and *www.crossmyheartprayerteam.blogspot.com*. As always, I thank God for bringing us together through this story. Wishing you abundant blessings,

Debby

Questions for Discussion

1. Why was Ted determined to shut Stephanie out of his life? When did their relationship finally heal?

2. Compare Brody's childhood to Stephanie's. What did they both lack growing up? How did that affect them?

3. What was the significance of the maritime bell?

4. Why did Stephanie hesitate to take *The Upton Queen* onto the lake? What happened that forced her into the boat again?

5. How did Brody turn the pain in his past into something positive?

6. What did you learn about the Army Wounded Warrior program? Can you see how the AW2 advocates help the injured throughout their recuperation and, in fact, as long as they need assistance? How can you reach out to a wounded soldier in your area?

7. Why did Stephanie feel responsible for Hayden's death? Who else in the story struggled with guilt?

8. Was Brody too antagonistic toward Ted or were his suspicions justified?

9. Did you understand the villain's motivation? Was the villain suffering from PTSD, and if so, would counseling have helped?

10. Do you think Stephanie and Ted reconciled with their father? Why had he been so distant for so many years?

11. What did Brody and Stephanie both learn about God's forgiveness and mercy? Have you held on to a pain in your past that needs to be healed? Have you turned to the Lord and asked His help?

12. What was the significance of Brody's artwork? Why had he stopped drawing and what happened to cause him to begin sketching again?

13. Why did Stephanie feel responsible for her brother? Did you agree with the doctor's advice?

14. Although Hayden was his mother's favorite, Keith was the son who took care of her in her need. How was Keith able to forgive his mother?

15. What was the significance of the last two secrets revealed in this story?

REQUEST YOUR FREE BOOKS!

2 FREE RIVETING INSPIRATIONAL NOVELS PLUS 2 FREE MYSTERY GIFTS

YES! Please send me 2 FREE Love Inspired® Suspense novels and my 2 FREE mystery gifts (gifts are worth about $10). After receiving them, if I don't wish to receive any more books, I can return the shipping statement marked "cancel." If I don't cancel, I will receive 4 brand-new novels every month and be billed just $4.74 per book in the U.S. or $5.24 per book in Canada. That's a savings of at least 21% off the cover price. It's quite a bargain! Shipping and handling is just 50¢ per book in the U.S. and 75¢ per book in Canada.* I understand that accepting the 2 free books and gifts places me under no obligation to buy anything. I can always return a shipment and cancel at any time. Even if I never buy another book, the two free books and gifts are mine to keep forever.

123/323 IDN F5AN

Name _____ (PLEASE PRINT) _____

Address _____ Apt. # _____

City _____ State/Prov. _____ Zip/Postal Code _____

Signature (if under 18, a parent or guardian must sign)

Mail to the Harlequin® Reader Service:
IN U.S.A.: P.O. Box 1867, Buffalo, NY 14240-1867
IN CANADA: P.O. Box 609, Fort Erie, Ontario L2A 5X3

Are you a current subscriber to Love Inspired Suspense books and want to receive the larger-print edition?
Call 1-800-873-8635 or visit www.ReaderService.com.

* Terms and prices subject to change without notice. Prices do not include applicable taxes. Sales tax applicable in N.Y. Canadian residents will be charged applicable taxes. Offer not valid in Quebec. This offer is limited to one order per household. Not valid for current subscribers to Love Inspired Suspense books. All orders subject to credit approval. Credit or debit balances in a customer's account(s) may be offset by any other outstanding balance owed by or to the customer. Please allow 4 to 6 weeks for delivery. Offer available while quantities last.

Your Privacy—The Harlequin® Reader Service is committed to protecting your privacy. Our Privacy Policy is available online at www.ReaderService.com or upon request from the Harlequin Reader Service.
We make a portion of our mailing list available to reputable third parties that offer products we believe may interest you. If you prefer that we not exchange your name with third parties, or if you wish to clarify or modify your communication preferences, please visit us at www.ReaderService.com/consumerchoice or write to us at Harlequin Reader Service Preference Service, P.O. Box 9062, Buffalo, NY 14269. Include your complete name and address.

LISDIR13R

ReaderService.com

Manage your account online!

- Review your order history
- Manage your payments
- Update your address

*We've designed
the Harlequin® Reader Service
website just for you.*

Enjoy all the features!

- Reader excerpts from any series
- Respond to mailings and
  special monthly offers
- Discover new series available to you
- Browse the Bonus Bucks catalog
- Share your feedback

Visit us at:

ReaderService.com